Becoming Felix

Other Avon Camelot Books by
Nancy Hope Wilson

BRINGING NETTIE BACK
THE REASON FOR JANEY
A WHIFF OF DANGER

NANCY HOPE WILSON was born in Boston and grew up in suburban Massachusetts and rural Vermont. She is a graduate of Swarthmore College and the Harvard Graduate School of Education, and she has taught in day care centers, elementary schools, high schools, nursing homes, and human service agencies. She also worked for five years as a carpenter. Her other books include novels *Bringing Nettie Back, The Reason for Janey*, and *A Whiff of Danger*, and a picture book, *Helen and the Hudson Hornet*. She lives in Amherst, Massachusetts, with her husband and two children.

NANCY HOPE WILSON

BECOMING FELIX

AN AVON  CAMELOT BOOK

AVON BOOKS, INC.
1350 Avenue of the Americas
New York, New York 10019

To my mother
With love and gratitude,
And to Jenckes Farm

Acknowledgments

Harold White, Jr., has been as important to this book as flour to bread. It was Hal's dairy farm that gave substance and texture to the story I wanted to tell. For eleven months of weekly visits, Hal welcomed me into his barns and fields, answered my endless questions, and—most important—put me to work. He taught me to milk, to bed stalls, to plow, to ted hay, to draw a calf's markings on the registration form. For the years of writing that followed, Hal generously offered both information and encouragement.

Farmer Cathy Shugg, her daughters, Kimberly and Sarah, and her border collie, Ben, also contributed invaluably to this book. The larger farm community helped me, too: the Jacque family, the Wentworth family, the Wagners, Bill Eddy, Richard McIntire and Raymond Duda, Hillary Cochrane, and Dick Allen.

I am deeply indebted to many others. For musical guidance: to Beth Bryant, inspired musician and inspiring teacher. For other crucial consultations: to Tom Reney, Sue Fullam, Laura Vogel, Rosie and Roger Wilson, and Leslie Sternberg and Judith Lytel. For perceptive and supportive critique of the many evolving versions of this story: to Cynthia Stowe, Jessie Haas, Michael Daley, Lorraine Ryan, Wini Luhrmann, Jean Rice Shaw, Lenore Blegvad, and my editor, Beverly Reingold. For moral support when I needed it most: to Olivia Dreier, Hilde Cohn, Mary Noland, Andrea Reber, Del Ames, and—always—Caleb, Hannah, and Nick.

1

JJ emerged from the woods into the hilltop pasture, swinging a big white grain bucket. The heifers were nowhere in sight. He'd have to send Sketch to round them up. She'd already scooted under the electric fence, and now turned to bark at him.

"Not yet, girl," he called. "Settle down."

He knew he was asking a lot of her. Both the other groups, the big calves and the yearlings, had been waiting for their grain. The border collie had been deprived of her favorite job, and was doubly impatient to get to work. She ran around the huge metal bin where JJ would dump the feed, then stopped to bark again, bowing on her forepaws with her tail wagging high.

"Yeah, I know," JJ answered, "but just wait for Steven." He looked back the way he'd come. "Steven?" he called.

"I'm resting!" Steven was invisible through the trees, but

JJ could tell he was just below the last steep climb. Steven sighed loudly. "Have to gather my strength, you know, for the charge to the summit!"

JJ smiled, but he felt a little guilty. He always forgot that his own daily routines were exercise for his friend.

"Lie down, Sketch," he commanded, and Sketch reluctantly obeyed.

JJ set down the bucket and went to stand by the big turtle rock. From there he could see the whole farm, tucked into the hollow between one hill and the next. From there, the white house, red barn, twin silos—even the scattering of sheds—seemed to grow out of the land as naturally as the ancient cider-apple trees that spilled their branches down the slope above the barn. The milk cows were splotches of black and white in the pasture across the river. Everything was as it had always been. He took a long, deep breath, full of the passing summer and the last ripened hay.

"Phew!" Steven puffed. He was at the edge of the woods, leaning against a tree. "Steep," he said, and lolled his tongue dramatically. He was red-faced and sweaty, despite his shorts and tank top, and his bangs were plastered across his forehead in black streaks.

Sketch barked again.

"Okay, girl," JJ said, and Sketch stood up, too tensely alert now to bark.

Steven suddenly revived. "Hey, let me say it. I like this part."

"Be my guest," JJ said.

Steven went over to the electric fence, a single strand of wire, and looked Sketch right in the eye. "Shhhhh!" he commanded loudly, and Sketch took off in a streak of black and white.

JJ grabbed the bucket and ducked under the fence. He shook the grain noisily. "Come, boss!" he called in his deepest voice. "Come, boss!"

"Hey," Steven said, "why do you call them 'boss,' anyway?"

JJ shrugged. "Never thought about it," he said. He called cows the way he'd heard them called all his life.

Steven laughed. "I've heard of 'Yes, boss' and 'No, boss,' but never 'Come, boss.'"

JJ only half smiled. "Come, boss!" he called again, but now it didn't sound right.

The bottom of the feed bin had long ago rusted out, so JJ just poured the grain on the ground inside it. Then he stood looking across the pasture to where Sketch had disappeared down the other side of the hill. He listened for the rumbling of hooves, but heard only the buzzing silence of a late-summer afternoon. Then there was the high cry of a hawk. He shaded his eyes to look for it. "Red-tail," he said aloud.

Steven was reaching for the bucket. "Hand me that drum, will ya?"

JJ grinned. "Come and get it."

"Yeah, right. In my new school sneakers? Look at all those cow pies, man!"

JJ laughed and tossed the bucket under the fence. As it

bounced with a hollow ring, he heard the heifers coming, pounding up the hill at a run. They appeared over the rise, already slowing down. JJ counted them. Only eight. There was a lone straggler, but Sketch would bring her in. These were the older heifers, all bred now and due to calve by spring.

"Now, which one's Claire again?" Steven asked.

JJ pointed. "The blackest one, with the white blaze on her forehead." Claire was JJ's heifer, nearly two years old. He'd raised her himself—groomed and pampered her, and shown her for ribbons at 4-H fairs.

"She's gotten big," Steven said.

JJ laughed, thinking how hugely Claire would bulge by spring. "You think *that*'s big?"

"She's still growing?"

"Well, you know, she finally settled—I mean, got pregnant." JJ had been worried, actually. It had taken several costly breedings for Claire to settle.

"Pregnant?" Steven sounded surprised. "How'd you manage that? I thought you only kept females."

"Well, yeah, but they have to have a calf to freshen—you know, give milk." If Claire hadn't settled, she'd have been useless on a dairy farm.

"Milk—oh yeah, right. But, so, if they're all females, how—" Steven stopped. He actually blushed a little. "Never mind." He picked up the white bucket, holding it upside down like a drum. He went back toward the woods. "Now all I need is a couple of sticks."

If Steven had finished his question, JJ would have answered it, but he was just as glad not to have to. Whenever he explained things to Steven, ordinary words—like *udder* and *teat*—and ordinary practices—like artificially inseminating a cow—seemed to turn embarrassing and strange. Here he was, just graining the heifers the way he'd done all his life, when suddenly even "Come, boss" seemed weird.

Now the last heifer galloped up, wide-eyed. Sketch tore after her, enjoying the chase too much.

"Steady, Sketch," JJ commanded. "Good girl. Now go lie down."

Heads in the bin, the heifers huffed and snuffled till the sweetness of pasture breath mixed with the sweet smell of grain. JJ stood among them so that Claire, intent on her grain, could still jostle him.

Mom and Dad had given JJ a newborn calf about a year after Gram had given him Gramp's old clarinet. He'd named the black calf Claire Annette.

JJ curved his arm over Claire's back to scratch her other side. Early next May she would calve and freshen, and so join the milk herd. Even before he turned thirteen, JJ would be a true dairy farmer.

Suddenly there was a drumroll. Steven was sitting on the turtle rock with a stick in each hand and the bucket upside down between his knees. He started with a slow, simple beat: *bah* chicka, *bah* chicka, *bah* chicka, *bah*. Then he burst into a swing rhythm like the ones Ms. Byron had been teaching them at the end of sixth grade: chicka *bee*da, chicka *bah*da, chicka beeda beeda *bah*da.

When JJ ducked back under the fence, Steven stopped abruptly. He'd already found a good, thick stick, and he handed it to JJ. Automatically, JJ's fingers placed themselves the way they would on his clarinet.

"Join me," Steven said, and resumed his drumming.

JJ could just *hear* the clarinet wail upward over the beat, then spiral down again. He tried to imitate it with his voice: "Ooweeeee, a–doodly–oodly–oodly," and he actually made it through a few bars before they both burst out laughing.

JJ sat down. "My singing's pathetic."

"Yeah, but you're great at clarinet." Steven slapped him on the back. "You're the new Benny Goodman. At least that's what Ms. Byron thinks."

"Yeah, right. What about you?"

"I'm great, too," Steven said. "What can I say? We're both great."

JJ lay back in the grass. "I sure didn't practice much this summer." Playing bits of Mozart for Gram wasn't exactly practicing.

"Jeez, that's *all* I did." Steven put the bucket aside and slid down to lean against the rock. "Except for sleep, of course."

Steven's mom worked at the state university in Hampton, about an hour to the east, and his dad worked at Berkshire Hospital, about an hour to the west. That was why, a year ago, the Lerners had moved from Hampton to this little town of West Farley, Massachusetts. Steven spent summer weekdays sleeping late, watching videos, and playing his drums to jazz CDs and to his parents' old rock-and-roll records. On weekends, he still spent a lot of time in Hampton. There was synagogue on Saturdays, JJ knew, and then something Steven called Sunday school, but when it came to religion, JJ didn't pry. He'd never known a Jewish kid till Steven, not that it made any difference. Steven was Steven.

Now JJ watched the red–tail soar off toward the south. Soon there would be others, and then the geese would come from the north, trailing the cold behind them.

Steven seemed to be watching the sky, too. He took a deep breath. "Seventh grade," he said. "Amazing. In my old town, I'd be going to junior high."

"Scary," JJ said.

West Farley had voted several times to keep its local school "K through 8." There'd always been just one class per grade, and JJ couldn't imagine what the huge regional school would be like. Those endless bus rides. And no Ms. Byron. "Hope she starts band right away," he said.

Steven was clearly on the same wavelength. "Ms. Byron? Are you kidding? By next Friday, she'll recruit the kids who can still barely toot, and then she'll hand out a schedule of concerts, including a few for national TV and maybe even one at the White House. I can see the headlines now." Steven gestured grandly into the air. " 'Little Podunk Band Wows the President.' "

JJ smiled. Because of Ms. Byron and band, he wasn't entirely sorry to see the summer go. "My gramp played clarinet for the governor once," he said. "But classical, of course. Gram has a picture of him wearing a tuxedo."

"Strange," Steven said.

JJ felt the tiniest tightening of every muscle. "What's so strange about that?"

"Oh, I don't know. Just, your gramp must've been real good. So why'd he stow his clarinet in the attic and milk cows till he dropped dead? Seems like kind of a waste."

JJ sat up. "You sound like my brother: 'Farming's for fools.' "

"But Ray's not a musician, is he? I meant—"

"Can you hand me that bucket?" JJ stood up and got the bucket himself. "Milking time," he said.

Sketch ran ahead down the steep path. JJ followed her without looking back.

How could Steven call Gramp's life a waste? And why did JJ even care? Ray and Liz had grown up with Gramp, but by the time JJ'd come along, Ray was twelve, Liz was ten, and Gramp had already died after a third heart attack. The farm had been passed along to Dad, and Gramp's name—Felix John Jaquith—had been passed along to JJ. Underneath his nickname, JJ was Felix. "It means *happy*," Gram often said. But to JJ the name felt large and awkward, like the old tuxedo in the attic. Whenever he tried it on, it just didn't fit.

"Hey, wait up!" Steven called when they reached the open field. JJ slowed down, but Steven still had to run. He was breathing hard when he came up beside JJ. "Are you mad or something?"

JJ shrugged. "Nah." How could he explain to Steven what he didn't understand himself? He needed to be alone for a while, quit feeling strange to himself. "I'm just late for chores," he said.

Steven's mountain bike was leaning against the house, and Steven headed for it.

"Don't you want to help in the barn?" JJ asked. He almost kept a straight face.

Steven's nose seemed to wrinkle automatically. He laughed. "Yeah, right. Dream on." He straddled his bike. "Hey, you want to come over tomorrow, jam a bit?"

"Nah. Busy," JJ said. He only wanted to get back to work. Sketch was circling him, impatient to go bring in the milk herd.

"But tomorrow's supposed to be a holiday," Steven said.

"Yeah. Labor Day. A day of labor." That was Dad's line, and JJ chuckled the way Dad would.

"What a drag," Steven said. "Well, see you on the bus, then," and he shoved off down the bumpy dirt driveway.

2

Band did meet the first Friday of school. Every fall a record number of fourth-graders started instruments, and a record number of fifth-graders were ready to join the band. JJ figured there must be fifty kids in band this year—almost a quarter of the school.

Ms. Byron had cut her hair really short in front and let it grow long in back, but she still wore loose-fitting clothes and that comfortable smile.

"Trumpets," she was saying from her seat at the piano. "See that *Sfzp*? Remember what *Sfzp* means?"

"Sforzando piano," someone answered.

"Right! So let me hear that hard attack. Then come right down so we can hear the clarinet. And Steven. Measure 25: it's one, two-dah, three—not one, two, three-dah. Got it?"

JJ moistened the clarinet reed with his tongue and

caught Steven's eye. On the first few pieces, JJ'd felt like a clumsy beginner again, stumbling into his entrances and losing his place on the page whenever he glanced at Ms. Byron. But this one was "The St. Louis Stomp," an old swing number they'd learned last spring. He and Steven had played it a few times over the summer, and now, from opposite ends of the band, they still seemed to be playing together.

"Okay," Ms. Byron said. "Practice is magic. Let's start at measure 19." She stood up from the piano bench and raised her arms. She waited for complete stillness. "And at 43, JJ, you be ready to wail."

JJ's eyes didn't even flicker, and not a muscle twitched, but a familiar tingling rushed through him, from the pit of his stomach to the tips of his ears.

Ms. Byron held still a second longer. Then—"One, two, ready, play"—and her arms dove into the downbeat.

The trumpets got the sforzando piano and Steven got measure 25, and the music built till it carried JJ right off into his solo. He didn't exactly wail, but after the final drumroll he looked over at Steven, who was grinning back at him. They both laughed. Last year's star musicians—a drummer, a sax player, and a trumpet player—had all been eighth-graders. They'd graduated. Now it was obvious who this year's stars would be.

"Okay, folks," Ms. Byron said. "Not bad for a first rehearsal."

Immediately, there was talk and commotion as kids pushed back chairs and opened instrument cases.

"Now, wait just a minute," Ms. Byron commanded. "A few announcements." The noise settled to whispers and murmurs. "We meet every Friday, so don't forget your instruments. Individual lessons start Monday. Check the bulletin board. Now I want to try something new—hey, Mark, pay attention, okay?—I want to try something new this year if there's enough interest." JJ saw her catch Steven's eye, and then she looked straight at JJ. "I want to start a jazz band this year."

"All *right*!" Steven burst out, and JJ and Steven exchanged a high-five sign.

"We'll meet after school once a week. Let's see a show of hands."

JJ raised his clarinet in the air, but he noticed Steven hesitating.

"I can't do Tuesdays," Steven told Ms. Byron.

That was news to JJ. What was Steven doing on Tuesdays?

"Oh, sorry, didn't I say that? Wednesdays. We'll meet after school on Wednesdays. Hands again?"

This time, Steven's hand shot up.

"What do you mean by jazz?" a flutist asked.

Ms. Byron smiled at him. "We'll do some swing—like that last number—and some bluesy stuff, and some jazzy rock, even. Remember 'Rock Around the Clock' last year?—more like that."

The flutist nodded, but kept his hand down.

Ms. Byron made a quick count. "Sixteen. Great! Now, get one of these permission slips signed. We'll start next

Wednesday." The noise immediately increased again, but this time she just raised her voice over it. "Art's meeting in here this year, so fold up your chairs and put them in that rack over there."

Band rehearsed in one corner of the cafeteria, which also served as gym, auditorium, and classroom.

JJ jumped up and went around the commotion to Steven.

"All *right*!" Steven said, and hit the snare drum before he took it off its stand. "A jazz band! Can you believe it?"

"I figured I could get a ride home with you?"

"No sweat. It's perfect. My mom goes right by here on her way home from work."

"My dad, too, but not till late."

"Well, like I said—no sweat."

"Good," Ms. Byron said, coming up behind them. She was holding out some music. "Here, you two. Take a look at these." The notes in one piece had been written out by hand—Ms. Byron had already transcribed it for clarinet. "I was counting on you two," she said as she walked away. "Can't have a jazz band without a drummer and a soloist." She turned. "So, JJ, work on that 'Memories of You' there for your lesson on Monday."

JJ had to go put away his clarinet and fold his chair, but then he helped Steven take down the drums. "So what's on Tuesdays?" he asked.

"Oh," Steven said. "Have to go to Hampton." He headed for the storage closet with the bass drum.

JJ took down the cymbals. For Steven, going to Hamp-

15

ton meant going to synagogue. But *three* days a week? Services, Sunday school, and now what? JJ tried to imagine someone going to church three days a week. It would seem a little scary, sort of fanatic. But maybe it was different for Jews.

"So!" Steven said as he came back. He picked up the beater for the bass drum, which was activated by a foot pedal and a spring. "You want to come over tomorrow? I'll get home from temple by two." He pressed the pedal with his hand, so the beater thumped on JJ's back. "We've gotta jam, man!"

"Can't tomorrow," JJ said. "We're going to an auction."

"Like antiques, you mean?"

"Nah. Cows."

"Cows? They auction cows?"

"When a farm goes under, yeah." They took the beater and the cymbals to the closet and went back to fold the stands. "This time it's Lindy Hamilton's," JJ said. "Well, I mean Ham's—he's her grandfather."

Steven shrugged. "Don't know her."

"Lindy," JJ prompted. "Eighth-grader last year. On our bus."

"You mean Lipstick Lindy? *She* lives on a farm?"

"Yeah. Until tomorrow, anyway."

While Steven took the stands away, JJ knelt to roll up the little square of carpet from under the drums. He had wondered why Lindy wore makeup to school. She never wore it at 4-H, and it made her look fakey. But maybe that was the point: to Steven, at least, she hadn't looked like a farm girl. And what about JJ? Did Steven have any clue how often JJ showered, how often he changed, how carefully he kept chore clothes and school clothes separate, even in the wash—all to avoid being teased about smelling like manure? Now, without Lindy, JJ was the only farm kid in school. Did Steven have any clue how lonely that felt?

Steven was there again, reaching for the carpet.

"You know," JJ said, standing up and handing it over, "as of tomorrow, we'll be the very last dairy farm in West Farley."

Steven beamed and slapped him on the back. "Hey," he said. "Congratulations!"

The school bus pulled up by the Jaquiths' mailbox, and as the doors folded back, JJ nodded to the driver and stepped down into the warm smell of cows.

He heard a bus window slide open.

"See ya, jazz man," Steven called, and JJ lifted his clarinet in a weighty wave.

He got the mail from the box and headed up the short driveway. The mail was mostly bills and equipment catalogues, but near the bottom was a letter from Liz at vet school. Mom would save it till Dad got home, then read it aloud at supper.

The yard between house and barn was dirt and gravel, packed hard by the daily traffic of tractors and milk trucks, grain trucks and livestock trailers. Now, though, the swallows had it to themselves, and they were making the best of it. Dozens of them swooped down, skimmed silently over the ground, then darted suddenly upward. When JJ arrived among them, they chittered in circles around him in what felt like a welcome. Then they landed on the overhead wire and cocked their heads to look down at him.

A metal conveyor track leaned like a bulky ladder against the high gable of the barn, waiting to carry the last hay bales up to the huge storage area under the roof. The storage area was called a mow, and until Steven had asked, JJ'd never wondered why this *mow* rhymed with *cow*. Mow; come, boss—it was all just farm talk.

With a burst of chatter and a purply flash of wings, a bunch of swallows dove into the mow, where their nests lined the eaves. JJ stopped by the bottom of the conveyor to whistle for Sketch.

There was no sign of her. Mom and Ray must be off somewhere, baling hay or bringing in firewood. These days, farms couldn't survive on milk alone. Mom had seeded extra acreage to hay and now sold bales by the truckload to stables and horse farms. Ray ran a cordwood business and a snowplowing service—and there was always the maple syrup. "Diversifying," the government called it, but Dad still needed his construction job.

JJ turned toward the house. Gram would be home.

In the musty back hall off the kitchen, he sat down amid the jumbled boots and jackets, the jugs of maple syrup left out for the occasional customer. Gram did not allow shoes—even school shoes—on her sacred kitchen floor.

He could hear water running and Gram humming to herself. As he padded into the kitchen, he dropped the mail on the table.

"Letter from Liz," he announced, and went to set his clarinet on the old upright piano in the living room.

Gram was at the sink, peeling potatoes. He shuffled up beside her and put his arm around her shoulders to give her a quick squeeze. Gram leaned a little into his hug, but kept right on humming and peeling. He'd grown past her height—five feet and one inch—some time ago, but it still felt rude to be taller than Gram.

"Want some help?" he asked, and grabbed a couple of cherry tomatoes from the basket on the counter.

Gram straightened her shoulders. "Do I look particularly decrepit today?"

Then she turned and smiled at him through the strands of white hair that had strayed from her bun. Some old people got wrinkly as they aged, but Gram's face seemed to get smoother and smoother, till now the skin across her cheeks was a soft, translucent pink. Only the finest, tiniest wrinkles showed around her eyes where her glasses magnified them.

"Thank you, dear, just the same," she said, and plopped a slippery peeled potato into a pan of cold water. "Now go change. Ray'll be back soon with another load of hay."

JJ had popped both tomatoes into his mouth, making the sweetness explode against his sealed lips. "Mmmm," he said as he crossed the kitchen. By the doorway he could swallow and speak. "Hey, guess what?"

19

He saw Gram's eyebrow go up as she slid another potato into the pan.

"Ms. Byron's starting a jazz band."

Gram turned now, her paring knife poised. "Jazz?"

"Yeah, well, sort of swing, really. There was this guy named Benny Goodman, and he—"

"Benny Goodman?"

"Yeah, he was—"

"JJ," Gram said. She rested both wrists on the edge of the sink. "Go find the cover to that Mozart record."

"Sure," JJ said. "Why?"

There was no question which record she meant. One side had Mozart's only clarinet concerto; the other, his clarinet quintet. There was other great music in Gramp's old collection, but that quintet was Gram's absolute favorite—and JJ's, too, by now. It rarely left the turntable, and JJ had to rummage around on the dusty shelves above to find the cardboard cover. There, smiling out from behind black-rimmed glasses, clarinet in hand, was Benny Goodman.

"You're kidding," JJ said. "He played classical?"

"Like an angel," Gram answered.

JJ smiled, because what came to his mind was a rusty feed-company sign nailed high on one of the silos: a yellow ear of corn with green wings. As a little kid, he'd decided the corn-angel was Gramp, still hovering over the farm—an earthly ear of corn in airy flight, a dairy farmer who loved Mozart.

Gram finished the last potato and gathered the peels for

the compost. "So, don't be telling *me* about Benny Goodman," she said. "We used to dance to that swing of yours. Play me some."

"I only just got the music."

"So this'll be practice."

JJ smiled. "And practice is magic."

He went to retrieve his clarinet and sat at the kitchen table, sucking on the reed while he assembled first key joint and second key joint, barrel and bell, mouthpiece and—last—the reed under the ligature.

Gram wiped the counters until JJ opened the music on the table.

"Here goes nothing," he announced.

Gram put down the sponge and faced him with both hands on the back of a chair.

JJ moistened the reed again, then played the melody of "Memories of You," swaying a little with the lilt of it. In the kitchen, the music sounded sweet, thickening the air like the smell of baking. Gram cocked her head and closed her eyes.

Then JJ hit the variations part and messed up. He laughed. "Told you so."

Gram was just opening her eyes. "Felix John Jaquith," she said. She turned toward the sink and took up the sponge again. "You're growing right into that name."

JJ thought of the tuxedo in the attic. It had been folded on top of the clarinet. A waste, Steven had called it.

"Gram?"

"What, dear?"

"Gramp *wanted* to be a farmer, right?"

Gram scrubbed at the counter so hard that when she finally spoke her voice jiggled. "Farming's what Gramp did," she said, "not who he was."

JJ started to ask what that was supposed to mean, but Gram had already added, "Now go get changed, or Ray'll be grumping at you."

3

JJ had just gotten to his room when he heard a tractor out on the road. That would be Ray. JJ could tell by the roughness of the engine noise that Ray was on Old John, an ancient John Deere tractor repaired and rebuilt since Gramp's time, but still good enough to pull a load of hay. For working the baler in the field, Mom used New John, still called new after twenty-five years.

JJ changed by the window so that he could watch the tractor turn in. It was Ray at the wheel, all right, but Mom rode the fender, so this was the last run of the day. The wagon jounced behind them, bales piled high above the high rails. Sketch stood balanced on top of the load, panting and gulping the air. She looked as if she were laughing.

JJ left his school clothes in a heap on the floor. If the unloading started without him, he'd likely get stuck at the bottom of the conveyor, heaving bales onto the track. He wanted to be the one at the top, grabbing each bale as Ray sent up the next. The mow was already crammed full from the first cutting in spring and the second in summer. As JJ wedged this third cutting under the eaves, he'd block his way back to the trap door. Then Mom would have to let him climb down the steep conveyor. She wouldn't have to watch.

As JJ searched for his barn sneakers in the jumble on the porch, he listened for the conveyor's motor. All he heard was Mom and Ray, sounding annoyed at each other again. Sketch bounded in, leapt up to lick JJ's face, rolled over for a belly scratch, and bounded back outside. Then Ray clomped up the steps, filling the doorway with his broad frame.

"Damn baler belongs in a junkyard," he muttered. Then he hollered over his shoulder, "I'm breaking for a cup of coffee." He paused just inside the door. There was grease on his cheek and hay in his beard. "Farming's for fools," he announced. "You got that, Squirt?"

"Sure," JJ said, and grinned.

But Mom was right behind Ray, and pushed past him into the dimness. She wasn't smiling. "A lot of fools in this family, then, Ray."

"Yeah, well . . ." Ray said, and came on into the room.

JJ could feel Mom stiffen. He jammed his feet into his sneakers and stood up.

"Hey," he said, "let's go unload, Mom. You send 'em up to me."

But Mom was folding her arms and glaring at Ray. "You're twenty-four years old, Raymond Jaquith. You can do what you want. I'm tired of your grousing."

"Yeah, sure. Do what I want." Ray sat down to untie his work boots. "Liz goes off—"

"Don't bring your sister into this. She *earned* that scholarship."

"Yeah, well, I may've flunked out of college—"

"You didn't flunk out, Ray. You quit."

"Have it your way, Mom, but I'm no genius, and even I can see that you can't farm this place alone."

"Hey," JJ protested, "what about me?"

"Yeah," Ray said, half smiling at Mom. "Get the Squirt here to fix that baler."

"It won't be long now," Mom said. She actually smiled at JJ, but he sat back down heavily.

The truth was obvious: he was just a tall, skinny kid. Ray was a man. Ray might curse the ancient farm machinery, but he could get it working again. He might call the cows dumb beasts, but he could take command of a half ton of balking heifer and lead her home from pasture. It would be a long time before JJ could do that.

Mom sat down on a crate of empty maple-syrup jugs. She looked at her hands for a long moment. JJ looked at them, too. They'd always been rough and callused, but when had those veins started showing?

"Ray," she said, still looking down, "you know how much we value all your hard work." There was a new tone in her voice—tired, sad. Why was she letting Ray get to her this time? She folded her hands. "But it won't do us any good for you to stick around here getting bitter. We'll hire someone if we have to."

Ray snorted and tossed his boots aside. "Oh, sure, Mom. Get real."

JJ knew that Mom knew that Ray was right: the milk already cost them more than they got for it. Dad had taken the construction job to bring in some money until— Until what? The price of milk went up? The price of feed and vets and electricity and gasoline went down? Dad had been working in Hampton for four years already.

Ray leaned back against the wall with exaggerated calm. "Mom, face it. I'm stuck here till we sell the herd."

JJ jumped up. "Ray! Cut it out! You're talking crazy! We're *never* selling out!"

Mom just sat there, looking steadily across at Ray. Her frizz of gray hair looked wild. "This family's been building that herd for five generations, Ray."

"Yeah. Breeding 'em fancy and feeding 'em fancy so they'll give more milk—exactly what every other farmer's been doing for generations, so now there's so much milk we can't get squat for it."

"Thank you, Raymond," Mom said, "but I don't need an economics lesson."

JJ stood looking from one to the other. Even standing over them, he felt small and useless. He plunked himself down on the bench again. "Well, *some*body's gotta raise milk."

"Sure, Squirt. The big places, with a few hundred cows

and no vet bills—if a cow gets sick, ffft!" Ray slapped one hand against the other. "Off she goes to slaughter."

Mom was quiet for a long moment. She and Dad had a friend who, when his own farm had folded, had hired on as a milker at one of those big dairies. It was a franchise, like a doughnut shop or something. The workers wore blue coveralls with the name of the company emblazoned on the back. The cows didn't even have names.

Mom shifted and stretched out her left leg stiffly, as if her bad knee hurt. JJ had to look away, because suddenly she seemed a lot older than fifty. Her cheeks sagged, and her chin seemed to quiver.

"Ray," she said, softly now. "It isn't a matter of logic, and you know it. Farmers have to farm. Your dad was born to it; I'm a transplant." She half laughed. "A suburban girl with a degree in English lit! But, either way, we *have* to farm. It's who we are."

Ray was picking bits of hay out of his socks. "Dad's building condos."

Mom leaned toward him. "But that doesn't change who he is."

Where had JJ just heard that? Gram had been talking about Gramp. *Farming's what Gramp did, not who he was.* But who was Gramp if not a farmer?

Ray tried to laugh. "So when do *I* get to be who *I* am?"

Mom looked at him steadily. "Soon as you figure out who that is, Ray. That's what I'm trying to tell you."

JJ felt invisible again. He slapped both knees, the way Dad would. "So are we unloading that hay, or not?"

Mom sighed. "It's getting late, J. Why don't you just go bring in the herd."

As JJ stepped outside and Sketch leapt to greet him, he heard Mom say wearily to Ray, "That boy's half your age and twice the farmer."

"Twice the fool, then," Ray muttered back.

4

Out in the yard, JJ crouched to rub Sketch's chest, but she pulled away and barked. Sketch was all business at milking time. She had work to do.

JJ smiled. "No question who *you* are, huh, girl?"

Sketch shot ahead, around the side of the barn and out the muddy lane.

JJ followed slowly. At each electric gate, he stopped to move the wire aside and clear the herd's way home.

What if Ray *did* leave?

The answer was simple: He just couldn't, that was all. Not until JJ was out of high school. Five years. Would that be enough time? In the spring, when Claire joined the herd, JJ'd be a dairy farmer, but when would he be able to fill Ray's shoes?

He walked along the ridge where the cows had worn a path through the side pasture. Sketch was way ahead by the heifer barn, which stood empty until winter. Half the herd—the nearly forty calves and heifers now out to pasture—would be sheltered there come November. Sketch wheeled around and came back to leap up onto JJ.

"Okay, girl, okay," he said, and he actually walked faster, past the heifer barn to the crossing at the curve in the road. He grabbed the plastic gate handle and immediately jumped back. "Aah!" He'd been zapped by electric fences plenty of times, but that heart-racing tingle was always a fresh surprise. He'd been thinking so hard he'd forgotten about the break in the handle—one more thing that needed fixing. He'd remind Ray about it.

No! He'd fix the gate himself. The idea went through him like another jolt of current. He would start right now to take Ray's place. So what if he was half Ray's age? Mom had called him twice the farmer.

All thirty-six milkers had come back across the river to wait by the roadside gate. Sketch ran madly about, scattering them so she'd have to round them up again.

"Bad dog, Sketch," JJ said, but he didn't make her lie down. Even Sketch needed to feel useful.

All the way back along the ridge, JJ followed the plodding cows, listening to the delicate tinkling of their heavy neck chains and thinking of jobs he could take on. All the machinery was pulled and powered by the farm's five tractors. JJ'd learned to drive a tractor the minute his legs had gotten long and strong enough to work the stiff clutch. There was no chance he'd be allowed to drive New John and run the most dangerous machinery—the mower, the hay baler, the corn chopper—but he could insist on driving the wagons: hitch a full one to Old John, drive it home, unhitch it, and drive an empty one back to the field. After the corn was in, he could drive the manure-spreader over the stubbly fields, fertilizing for next year's crop. In spring, he could drive the plow and the cultivator, turning the earth for new corn, and later the tedder, which turned the mown hay to dry it. Come next July, JJ would be thirteen, and Mom and Dad would see that he could handle the work.

Ray wouldn't leave before that—would he?

When the cows had lumbered into the barn, turned in at their accustomed stalls, and lowered their heads to their grain, JJ secured their neck chains to the metal stanchions.

Mom came up the center alley with the milking units hung on the squeaky cart. Steam billowed from a bucket of hot water around the draped hoses and dangling suction cups.

"Ray's gone off to fix that baler before dark," Mom said.

"No problem," JJ said. "I'm here."

"What about your homework?"

"Prokopy goes easy on us the first week."

"*Mr.* Prokopy," Mom corrected. "And what about practicing?"

"No lesson yet." JJ didn't mention the jazz band.

Mom considered for a moment. "Well," she said, "go prep Jet, then, will you?"

JJ smiled. *One, two, ready, play.* The milking had begun.

31

"Careful!" Mom called as JJ approached Jet.

"I know, Mom." Jet was the only cow in the herd who'd kick just to be nasty.

They spoke little after that. All JJ's life, the cows had been milked every morning and every evening. The routine was as familiar as breathing. JJ squatted and stood, squatted and stood, washing and disinfecting each cow's udder. Mom stood and squatted, stood and squatted, attaching and checking and removing the milking units. The vacuum pump pulsed in a steady beat, drawing the milk into the pipeline.

Mom would keep the herd in the barn till Dad got home. Then the two of them would walk up one line and down the other as Mom passed on the day's news: Gentle little Ivory was bred that morning. Gert's mastitis was clearing up—boy, that cow was sickly! And guess what? After all the nutritional analysis and the fancy new grain, the prize milker, May, refused to eat the stuff.

They'd confer and confide and chuckle, and then—together—they'd turn the cows out for the night.

Only then would Gram serve supper, no matter how late Dad had gotten home.

That night, Dad came home early. Ray had just gotten back from the field, and Mom and JJ were in the milk house, setting up the pipeline for the wash cycle.

"Good," JJ said when he heard Dad's pickup. "I'm starved."

They heard Dad speak to Ray. Then the aluminum door swung open and Dad came up the steps into the milk house. Ray followed right behind him, his hands jammed into his pockets. Except for the beard and the sullen expression, Ray looked just like Dad—the same broad face, the same ruddy cheeks.

"Might as well start out with the bad news," Dad said, and JJ's stomach turned over.

Dad leaned on the silver bulk tank that took up most of the room. He looked across at Mom, but she just attached another hose to the wash valve. "Have to work Saturdays," he said, "starting tomorrow."

Ray swore and kicked the wall.

"But what about Ham?" JJ asked. Not showing up for the Hamilton auction would be like missing an old friend's funeral.

Dad took off his engineer's cap and smoothed one hand over his thinning hair. His forehead was pale above the hat line, and his bald spot looked white and exposed. "Ham'll understand," he said. "He'll have to."

Mom just turned to Dad. "Still behind schedule, Ed?"

Dad nodded and put his hat back on. "Foolish foundations went in so late, now it's a race against winter."

"Yeah," Ray said, "sort of like the corn harvest."

Mom glared at him and separated her words. "We can manage the corn harvest, Ray."

JJ spoke to Dad. "No problem, Dad. Cause this year I can drive the wagons, right?"

Dad smiled at him. "Maybe so."

Ray left them with a slam of the door.

Dad caught Mom's eye. "Rough day?"

Mom just shrugged and smiled. "You know how it is," she said. "One thing after another."

"Which reminds me," JJ said. "Have we got a new gate handle somewhere?"

Dad looked at him curiously. "In the blue toolbox, I think."

"Got zapped by the one at the crossing," JJ said. "I'll fix it before supper."

"Well," Dad said, "I guess that's fine. Don't forget to cut the juice!" He put out his arm to usher Mom up the steps to the barn. "Now, if you'll excuse me, young man"—he yanked at the bill of JJ's cap—"got to go see to my cows."

As JJ left to look for the blue toolbox, he could hear Mom begin reporting the day's news. He had a feeling she wouldn't mention her argument with Ray.

5

JJ usually slept late on Saturday mornings, but this time he got up at six o'clock to help with the milking as if it were a weekday. When he got to the barn, Dad was just leaving for work.

"Great timing," Dad said, and handed him a milking unit. "You give my best to Ham."

When the milking was done, the calves fed, the cows turned out to pasture, Gram served breakfast. Then, after cleaning the barn, Mom and Ray and JJ all showered and changed. It was strange, driving to Ham's smelling like soap.

Already, the Hamiltons' farm didn't look like a farm. There was a huge yellow-and-white tent set up in front of the barn. The side pasture had become a parking lot full of pickups with livestock trailers, and the back field was a huge display of old machinery—no older, JJ noticed, than their own at home.

There were rows of folding chairs under the tent, and Ray went straight to claim some seats near the back. Front seats were for buyers.

JJ got one of the little booklets that listed every animal for sale. He checked all the bred heifers. Lindy's Star and JJ's Claire had been in 4-H shows together. Star wasn't listed. JJ smiled. Lindy was hanging on.

JJ stood around with Mom for the greetings and small talk with other farmers. People had come up from Connecticut and down from Vermont, but there were very few faces JJ didn't recognize. Even Ernie Adams had shown up, bent over his walker. He wasn't that old, but he was already a legend. He'd always farmed alone, and even though both knees had given out some years ago, he crossed to his barn on that walker and milked his nineteen cows, leaning on a hoe. JJ had seen him: bent double from the waist, feet splayed out like a new calf's, back arched grotesquely so he could reach a sagging udder.

"Haven't seen Ed," he said to Mom, and she had to explain one more time why Dad wasn't there.

"Well, Catherine," Ernie Adams said, "you hold on, now." He had greasy black hair and a sharp, pocked face, but he smiled affectionately at Mom as he nodded toward JJ. "You've got sons. You'll do fine."

The auctioneer tapped the microphone. "All right," he said. "Let's get started."

The murmur of voices surged for a minute while sentences were finished, responses given.

The auctioneer leaned over the microphone in his

broad-rimmed brown hat. "Now, first," he said, "I want the family to come stand up here."

After a little scurrying, all the Hamiltons—brothers, sons, wives, and kids—stood side by side in front of the barn. Lindy was there between Ham and her dad. Her dark hair was pulled back into a neat ponytail. She smiled awkwardly as her little brothers tried to make rabbit ears behind her head.

"These are the folks responsible for this fine herd of cattle," said the auctioneer. "Let's give 'em a hand."

JJ clapped with the crowd, but was relieved when the auctioneer let the Hamiltons go back to the barn.

As the first cow was led out into the pen, JJ skirted the tent to enter the barn through the side door.

"Hi, JJ," Lindy's mother called. She was grooming the next cow with a curry comb. "Lindy's out back."

JJ headed for the ell that extended from one side of the barn. He was halfway there before his eyes adjusted to the dimness. Familiar as it was, this barn always smelled strange. For years now, Ham had kept his milk herd inside all year, feeding them some mixture of fermented "haylage" and grain. No green pasture. No sunshine. "That's not farming," Dad had snapped at first. Later he'd shrugged and added, "But neither is building condos."

The heifers were all in their stanchions, each with a number tag stuck to the hollow between hipbone and tail. Lindy was brushing Star, leaning heavily into every stroke. She didn't look up till JJ said hi.

"I thought you weren't selling her," he said.

Lindy shrugged. "I can't decide. If I do, the money's mine, but . . ." She paused. "I've never in my life spent a day without cows." Her voice cracked a little, so she laughed.

JJ scratched Star's flank. "Me, neither," he said.

"But what am I gonna do when Star freshens? Get up every morning to milk one cow?"

"If the calf's a heifer, you could sell Star and raise the calf."

"And if it's a bull?" Bull calves were the hardest part of dairying—sent off as soon as they were born, to be auctioned for meat.

Lindy turned away to brush Star's neck. "So, what do *you* think, J? Should I sell her?"

JJ couldn't imagine Lindy without Star. Nor could he imagine this whole barn standing empty. "Boy, I don't know," he said. Would one pampered heifer keep this place a farm? "I mean, well, it's up to you."

Lindy laughed again. "Good old JJ," she said. "You make it sound so simple."

JJ felt stung. "Nah," he said. "Not simple." The opposite, really. Like JJ's sister, Liz, Lindy always seemed to know exactly what she was feeling. When strong feelings hit JJ, he just got confused and tongue-tied. "Sorry," he said.

Lindy looked at him then. "Hey," she said, "I didn't mean . . ." She dropped her arms and leaned back against the heifer next to Star. She looked at the floor and kicked at the sawdust. "I guess I just envy you. Your folks would *never* quit."

JJ kept his voice even. "But Ray might."

"Oh, come on, J. Ray's *always* griping. That doesn't mean anything."

"Maybe so." JJ hoped she was right. "You want any help?" he asked.

"Nah." Lindy laughed again as she went back to brushing Star. "This is only the tenth time I've groomed her this morning."

There was too long a silence. "Okay," JJ said. "I guess . . . Well, good luck, okay, Lindy?"

"Yeah," she said. "Thanks, J."

"Well, see ya," he said. "Let me know if you need anything."

Lindy laughed. "Like a whole new life, you mean?"

JJ tried to smile, but he needed to get out of there, and there was no way to leave without turning his back on Lindy.

The Hamilton herd was bigger than the Jaquiths', and it took hours to auction a hundred cows: bring each one out, turn her in the pen, read out her breeding history and her milking records, rattle some mumbo jumbo as the bids came in. Even Ray was strangely fascinated, and he and JJ got into a game of guessing what each animal would sell for.

There was food for sale on the Hamiltons' porch, and JJ was just coming back with another round of hot dogs when the auctioneer announced, "Now, folks, this next animal is lot 94. She's not in your catalogue, but she's a fine heifer, cared for like a baby, due to calve March 21."

39

"That's Star," JJ said as he handed Mom her hot dog. He looked around for Lindy, but didn't see her.

The auctioneer gave Star's background. "Okay," he said then. "Turn her one time, and here she goes."

The bidding started low.

"Six hundred!"

"Six fifty!"

JJ saw Lindy come out of the barn with a can of soda in her hand. She climbed up onto the fence that met the low side of the barn, and set her soda in the rain gutter at the roof line.

The bidding stalled at seven fifty. The auctioneer kept interrupting his assistant to make speeches about how great Star was. "Buy yourself rich right here!"

Star mooed.

"That's her way of saying please!"

"Seven seventy-five!" Mom shouted.

Ray turned so suddenly that he bumped her hard with his shoulder. "Mom!"

"Eight hundred," the other bidder called.

JJ looked closely at Mom, but her face didn't offer a clue. "Eight twenty-five," she called out.

Ray was protesting in a loud whisper. "The last thing we need . . ."

"Eight fifty!"—the other guy.

"Eight seventy-five!"—Mom again.

"Nine hundred."

Now Mom leaned back. She smiled at Ray, who shook his head.

Nine hundred was a good price, but the auctioneer wouldn't quit. "Got to be a better investment than most things on Wall Street! Now, come on! I'm running out of speeches!"

"Well, I hope so," someone called. "If you don't hurry up, she'll be calving!"

Amid the laughter, the bidding climbed again, and Star was sold for one thousand dollars. JJ looked over at Lindy. She was wiping her eyes on her sleeve. Her mother had come to stand next to her, but Lindy stayed there on the fence. Instead of watching as Star was led away, Lindy carefully took another sip of soda.

6

At supper that night, Dad got the full rundown on the auction. With commentary from Ray and JJ, Mom went over who had been there, and all the messages people had sent to Dad.

"Ernie Adams says to hold on," she said.

Dad laughed. "Talk about holding on! That man's amazing."

"He's nuts," Ray said.

Mom had noted in the buyer's catalogue the going price of every animal.

Dad frowned at the list. "Fall's a bad time to sell," he said.

"*Any* time's a bad time to sell," JJ said.

Ray jabbed his empty fork into the air. "Any time's a bad time to *buy*. And Mom was bidding."

Dad looked at Mom with his eyebrows raised.

She shrugged and smiled. "Lindy's heifer was going cheap to Sam White—from up in Marlboro, you know."

"Gentleman farmer." Dad chuckled. "You made him pay."

"Exactly," Mom said.

Then the phone rang.

"I'll get it," JJ said, already up.

It was Steven. "Hi, jazz man. Any good bargains?"

"Bargains?"

"You know, at the auction."

"Oh. No. I mean, we weren't buying."

"Huh? So why'd you go?"

"Look, Steven, can I call you back? We're eating."

"Oh, yeah. Sorry. I always forget how late you guys—but I just had to tell you. I got this new CD of old Benny Goodman. It has 'Memories of You' on it."

"Hey, great!" JJ glanced at his clarinet on top of the piano. He'd forgotten to practice.

"So you want to come over tomorrow? We'll be back from Hampton by two."

"Sure." Then JJ remembered: if the weather held, they'd be haying again tomorrow. He was hoping to start driving the wagons.

But Steven had already said, "Great! See you then. Bye."

When JJ got back to the table, Mom smiled at him. "You and Steven getting together tomorrow?"

"Depends," JJ said. "I'd rather help with the haying if—"

"Oh, don't worry," Mom said. "Dad's home—we won't need you, honey."

Why did she have to put it that way? JJ wasn't needed. "But I could drive the wagons," he said.

Dad laughed. "You have to let me do *something* around here!"

"Besides," Gram said, "you've got to practice for that jazz band."

"Jazz band?" Mom asked, and suddenly everyone was looking at JJ.

He looked down at his plate. "Ms. Byron's idea," he said. "It'll meet on Wednesdays—I mean, is that okay?"

"Sure," Dad said. He didn't even hesitate. "If you wait at Whitcomb's store, I can pick you up on my way through."

"Steven's mom'll give me a ride," JJ said. "I'll be home in time for milking."

"Either way," Dad said.

JJ excused himself and got up to clear his place. Maybe he shouldn't have agreed to go to Steven's. How would he ever be as important as Ray if he kept going off to play music?

The next morning, Gram's friends came by to take her to church. JJ hadn't been to church since Sunday school when he was little. Funny to think that Steven still had Sunday school.

JJ rode his bike to Steven's house. He didn't realize till he got there that Steven's parents would be home. Over the summer, he'd usually come on weekdays, when they were at work. Now the garage door was open, and both cars were parked facing out, like dragonflies that had landed only to take off again.

Instead of going to the kitchen door, JJ rang the front

bell. He heard some stirring inside, but then there was silence. He stared at the little tile on the door jamb. It had that funny Jewish writing on it, and he wondered what it said. Welcome? Keep out? He'd have to ask Steven sometime.

Maybe the doorbell didn't work. He thought of trying it again, but that might seem rude. He'd wait a little longer. He turned around on the doorstep to look off over Hillcrest Drive—six or seven houses and only young, planted trees.

This had all been part of the farm once. JJ could remember coming up here with Ray to put the yearlings out to pasture. Dad had sold the land to a developer and used the money to modernize the barn—put in the milking machine and the electric gutter cleaner and the silo unloader—all so Mom could manage without him.

Suddenly the Lerners' door opened behind JJ, and a clean smell like shampoo swooshed around him.

"Oh, hi, JJ. Come on in." Mrs. Lerner had frizzy, shoulder-length hair, and she wearing a crisp blouse and fitted jeans. "Steven!" she called as she crossed back toward the kitchen. She stopped at the bottom of the stairs and leaned on the post. "Steven? JJ's here!" She listened, looking up the stairs, then smiled back at JJ. "He's probably wired to his stereo. Go right on up."

JJ was still standing on the welcome mat. He looked down to be sure he'd changed into school sneakers. Then he wiped his feet before crossing the beige carpet to the carpeted stairs.

Mr. Lerner was just starting down, dressed in an old

sweat suit and running shoes. "Well, hi, JJ!" He stopped where they met midway. Mr. Lerner had a soft, short beard and soft, steady eyes. "So how's it going?" he said. "You like this new teacher?"

"Yeah. I guess he's okay." The seventh-grade teacher was hardly new, though. Both Ray and Liz had had Mr. Prokopy.

"Well, great to see you," Mr. Lerner said, and went on down the stairs, already jogging as he passed through the kitchen and spoke to Mrs. Lerner.

Steven's door was open. He was lying on his back on the bed, hands behind his head. He had on his big headset, which looked exactly like the ear protectors JJ wore around farm machinery—big cups on the sides of his head. Steven had his eyes closed, and was lolling his head from side to side. JJ watched him for a second, trying to guess what kind of music was playing. Something slow and smooth, but rhythmic, too, because every so often Steven would kick one foot, whisper-shout *"Pah!"*, then go back to lolling his head.

JJ swallowed a laugh. He set down his clarinet by the door and snuck slowly over to Steven's drum set. The sticks were right there on the snare. Just when he thought the next *pah* was coming, JJ pressed the foot pedal on the bass drum and hit both the snare and the big ride cymbal. Steven jumped off the bed so fast that the headset came unplugged and music filled the room.

"What the—"

JJ doubled over in laughter.

46

"Very funny," Steven said, but he was smiling as he shut off the music and sat back down on the bed. It took him only a second to recover. "Look, you've got to hear this." He took a CD out of its case and handed the case to JJ. The Benny Goodman Sextet.

"Guess what?" JJ said. "Benny Goodman played classical, too."

"Hunh." Steven didn't seem that interested. He pushed some buttons on the CD player. "Here goes."

"Memories of You" was simple and smooth at first, but then it went spiraling off into high-flying improvisation. JJ tried to follow every note, tried to imagine his fingers moving that fast, his breath lasting that long. He sat down on Steven's bed, and when he closed his eyes, the music seemed to swirl so close around him that he breathed it in with every breath. He got so airy and light he thought he might float right off with those high notes.

He opened his eyes in case Steven was watching him, but Steven looked pretty lost himself. He'd moved over to his drums and was playing along quietly with just the brushes. He stopped the CD at the end of the cut.

"Great, huh?"

"I'll never be *that* good," JJ said, but even as he said it, he was getting his clarinet, putting it together, and imagining that someday he'd play like Benny Goodman.

7

September had begun softly, with steady sun to ripen the feed corn. JJ'd been checking the ears in the field between his house and Steven's. The kernels puffed up, fatter and fatter, until they looked ready to explode. Then they shrank back and dimpled.

"Corn's ripe," JJ said. It was the second Saturday without Dad, and JJ was helping with the evening milking.

"I know." Mom stood up and arched her back. "And Ray says the harvester's set to go." She straightened and smiled. " 'Rehabilitated for another season' is what he actually said."

Corn silage was the mainstay of the milk herd's winter diet, a richer source of energy than even the best hay. Between mid-September and mid-October, about five acres of corn had to be chopped—stalks and all—in the field, brought home by the wagonload, and propelled up into the silos. All winter long, the feed was unloaded from the top down. When Ray'd been JJ's age, he'd had to climb way up there in the cold to fork silage into the chute. Now the electric unloader took care of that.

"So," Mom said, "we'll start tomorrow, when your father's here."

"And this year I'm driving the wagons, right?"

Mom was squatting with a milking unit and didn't even look up. "Dad's going to teach you tomorrow—but no unloading, JJ. That's dangerous machinery."

All *right*! JJ didn't say it aloud. He heard it in his head, the way Steven would say it: All *right*! Even Ray and Liz hadn't driven the wagons till high school.

But then, the next day, before the old two-row harvester had even chopped one wagonload, it jammed up and froze. Ray knew right away which part had given out, but there was no replacing it on Sunday.

JJ went over to Steven's again, after all. Jazz band had started, and Ms. Byron was already talking about having them perform in the winter concert.

It took Ray a few days to find the right part. "They call our machine obsolete," he announced. "Not just old—ob-solete!"

Then, on the ride home from the second jazz-band rehearsal, Mrs. Lerner was just cresting the big hill when she suddenly braked hard. "Oops," she said, and slowed to a crawl.

Ray was up ahead on Old John, heading home with a

wagonload of corn. Pale gold flakes fluttered by JJ's window like oversized confetti. They'd started the harvest without him.

Even though Mrs. Lerner had to go very slowly, JJ could tell that Ray was driving too fast. He was losing half the load in the wind.

"What *is* that, JJ?" Mrs. Lerner asked.

"Corn."

"Really? It doesn't look like corn."

"Well, we chop the whole plant—for silage."

Mrs. Lerner gave a little laugh. "Forgive my ignorance, JJ, but what's silage?"

"Oh, that's okay," he said. He liked being asked about the farm. Even Steven seemed to be paying attention. "It's the food we give the cows all winter—along with hay and grain, of course. We add an enzyme—sort of a preservative—to the chopped corn and then store it in those big silos. It ferments a little, but it's pressed down so hard by its own weight it doesn't get enough air to rot. That's the whole point of silos." JJ felt out of breath from saying so much at once.

"Ingenious," Mrs. Lerner said. She seemed to watch the wagon ahead with new interest.

"I'm just glad it's not the manure-spreader," Steven said.

JJ knew he was expected to smile—and he actually did—but suddenly he was eager to get out of the car.

Finally, Ray swung wide and turned in at the driveway. Mrs. Lerner pulled up by the mailbox.

"Thanks!" JJ called as he jumped out. If he hurried, he could start learning to drive the wagon on the next trip.

"Hey, jazz man!" Steven called.

JJ pretended not to hear.

"Hey, jazz man! You forgot something!"

JJ looked back. Steven was leaning out the window with JJ's clarinet.

"Oh, thanks. See ya."

JJ hurried up the drive, but stopped to watch as Ray positioned the wagon for unloading. Backing a tractor with any kind of trailer on it still seemed impossible to JJ—like trying to do a puzzle while looking in a mirror—yet Ray made it seem effortless.

Practice is magic, JJ thought.

Leaving Old John idling, Ray swung down to start up the machinery for unloading.

"Hey, Squirt!" he called. "Hurry up and change. You've got to bring in the herd."

"I want to drive the wagons!"

"Have to get home earlier for that." Ray revved the tractors, and the machinery roared.

"Hey, you forgot the enzyme stuff," JJ shouted, but Ray couldn't hear him.

JJ almost turned to go in, but letting the silage spoil would punish the whole farm. The bag of enzyme was right there by the shed, so JJ set down his things and went to scoop out a canful. He climbed up on the side of the wagon.

"Hey, get out of there," Ray shouted, but looked up

just as JJ was scattering the enzyme over the load. Ray turned away.

"And you're supposed to wear ear protectors!" JJ shouted, but he knew Ray couldn't hear him.

Gram wasn't in the kitchen. A record on the turntable was still going round and round with a scratchy click, so she probably hadn't gone far.

"Hi, Gram!" JJ called out.

There was a heaped basket of green tomatoes on the table. Gram had outwitted the first light frost by covering her garden with old sheets, but today she must have recognized that sharp, clear smell in the air. Gram never bargained with a real killing frost. These tomatoes would be wrapped in newspaper for a few weeks, emerging—magically ripe—long after the plants had shriveled.

"Gram?"

JJ went into the living room to deal with the record, wishing for the millionth time that they could get a decent stereo system.

A tiny shuffle behind him made him glance around. "Oh!" His heart skipped a beat, but it was only Gram, sitting there in the big easy chair. "Hi, Gram. You scared me!"

She smiled at him. "I'm here," she said.

"You want this record changed or what?"

Gram didn't answer right away, and he turned, record in hand. She was nodding and still smiling, but as if her mind were elsewhere. "Yes," she finally said.

Something felt very odd, but JJ wasn't sure what. "Gram, are you okay?"

Gram looked confused for a second, and JJ started toward her, but then she caught his eye and sat up straighter, and he stopped in the middle of the room. He was still holding the record, and felt suddenly foolish. What had he planned to do? Rush over and feel Gram's forehead? He just wished she didn't look so tiny in that huge chair.

He looked at the record: von Weber this time. Another of Gramp's favorites. He wouldn't mind hearing it himself while he got changed.

As he was putting it on the spindle, Gram spoke again. "I . . . can't find . . ." she said slowly.

"Can't find what?"

Gram started to answer, but stopped to think for a second. "Words," she said. "I can't find my words."

JJ's throat suddenly felt dry. There *was* something wrong. Of course there was. Gram never sat in a chair like that—just sat with her hands in her lap.

"Look, Gram," he said. "I'll be right back, okay?"

He went straight to the hallway and opened the big front door that no one ever used. "Ray!" he called through the screen door. The machinery was off now, but Ray didn't hear him, or at least pretended not to. "Ray! Come here!"

Ray was starting out on Old John to go back for another load. JJ pushed against the screen door, but had to stop to unlock it. He burst out in stocking feet and ran across the yard, waving both arms at Ray.

Ray stopped, but let the tractor idle and leaned forward over the steering wheel as if to say, This better be good.

"It's Gram!" JJ shouted.

Ray's scowl dissolved, and in one sweeping motion he shut off the tractor and swung down to stride toward the house.

JJ ran to keep up with him. "She's in the living room."

Ray went through the front door without stopping to take off his boots. They sounded harsh and frightening on the wooden floor.

Gram's eyes were closed.

Ray squatted down beside her chair. "Gram? Gram, are you okay?"

Ray's voice was so gentle that JJ felt tears sting his eyes, not even for Gram, but for the memories that only now rushed back to him: his big brother giving him piggyback rides, or putting wet grass over his scraped knee and securing it there with baling twine.

When Ray touched Gram's shoulder, she opened her eyes and smiled at him. "Hello, sweetheart," she said, and JJ saw Ray swallow hard.

"Gram," Ray said, "I'm going to get Mom." He stood up. "JJ'll stay here with you—right, Squirt?" Then he lowered his voice to JJ: "I'll call an ambulance from the barn."

There was a heavy silence after Ray clomped out. Gram seemed to be thinking, but JJ'd already heard the pickup tear down the driveway by the time she found her answer to Ray.

"Ambulance!" she said. "Nonsense!"

JJ smiled. Gram was still Gram. "You want to hear some music?" he asked.

She nodded, but as he went to start the record, she kind of grunted, "Unh unh."

He looked back at her. She was wiggling her fingers as if playing the clarinet.

When Mom burst into the house a short time later, JJ was playing the last bars of "Memories of You," and Gram was smiling with her eyes closed. Mom stopped in the living-room doorway; Ray was right behind her. They waited till JJ finished.

There were still flakes of corn leaves in Mom's hair, and her eyes were glossy with tears when she crossed the room to crouch by Gram. "Dorothea," she said. "How are you feeling?"

JJ saw the ambulance turn in then, and went out to meet it. He was still in his socks.

"She's in here," he said, and the ambulance team took over.

Gram gave them a hard time about riding on the stretcher, but consented when they let her sit up. They had put a little strap over her head to hold a tiny oxygen tube to her nose.

"I'm perf . . . I'm perf . . . I can walk," she protested.

Mom winked at JJ. "Tell Dad I'll call the minute we know anything."

JJ stood watching the ambulance turn onto the road,

sirens silent, but lights flashing. Mom followed in her car.

Ray went to turn off the tractor, and in the sudden stillness JJ realized the swallows had gone.

"Don't worry, Squirt," Ray said. "Whatever it is, Gram's fightin' it. Now go get changed, 'cause it's you and me against the chores."

8

It would be nearly an hour to the hospital, so they didn't expect to hear from Mom soon.

Ray didn't do the milking very often, and the cows were restless around him.

JJ realized he was telling Ray what to do: "That's Jet. You'd better tie her tail aside or she'll whack you one. Hey, Gert's ready, you know. Here, I'll get it."

They didn't talk about Gram.

Ivory, usually a sweetheart, kicked off the milking unit twice. "Dumb beast," Ray said.

"We ought to check her udder. Maybe something's wrong."

Sure enough, Ivory had a little sore on one teat. JJ milked that quarter by hand.

They'd just finished the milking when the barn phone rang.

JJ answered it. "Jaquiths."

"Gram's fine," Mom said. "Just fine."

JJ set down the bucket of milk he'd been carrying to the calves. "She's fine," he said to Ray, who had come up right behind him.

"It was a little stroke," Mom explained, "a tiny one. They call it a TIA. By the time they got her hooked up to the monitor, it was mostly over."

"A stroke," JJ said to Ray, "but tiny. She's fine."

Ray took a long, deep breath and blew it out hard. Then he grabbed the bucket of milk and went on back toward the calf hutches.

"They've got Gram on medicine already," Mom said, "and they're keeping her overnight." She laughed a little. "So now she's annoyed at me for bringing her here."

JJ smiled into the phone, but his throat felt too tight to speak.

"Are you there, JJ?"

"Yeah, Mom."

"So tell Dad I'm on my way. I'll fill in the details when I get there. Chores go okay?"

"Yeah. Fine, Mom." He wished she'd seen how he'd ended up in charge.

"Okay, J. Find yourselves some supper and save me some."

"Yup. Bye, Mom."

It felt strange, trying to cook in Gram's kitchen. Leftover chicken, some noodles, the last stringy broccoli from the garden. Whenever JJ had helped in the kitchen, Gram had been there, presiding. Now the air prickled with her absence, and he felt disrespectful, almost sneaky. The pans clanged too loudly; the water gushed too fast from the faucet.

Dad got home and headed straight for the barn, so Ray went out to tell him about Gram.

"Tell him to check that sore on Ivory," JJ said.

He set the table. Then he realized he'd set five places. He cleared two and rearranged the others to be evenly spaced.

When Dad came in, he caught JJ's eye for just a split second. "Don't worry," he said, "Gram's tough." Then he surveyed the kitchen and smiled brightly. "Hey, looks like you've fixed us a feast here. I'll just go wash up."

JJ could not remember a time when he and Ray and Dad had eaten together like that—just the three of them. The prickle in the air only made them lean closer around the table.

"So it's a stroke," Dad said.

"Yeah." JJ tried to remember Mom's every word. "They call it an AIT—no!—a TIA."

Dad and Ray chuckled. AIT was the official name for a breeder—artificial insemination technician.

"Well," Dad said. "TIA, AT&T—whatever it is, sounds like Gram'll be back in charge before long. And, hey! speaking of taking charge, great job tonight."

JJ sat taller. "No sweat, Dad."

"Glad you realized what was bothering Ivory, J. That's

half the skill of dairying, you know—catching little problems before they get big."

"Too late for that," Ray muttered.

Dad seemed determined to stay cheerful. "You started
chopping corn, I see."

"Three loads into the silo," Ray said.

"Which reminds me: you know what they're naming
this condo complex?" Dad grinned.

"Gross Gardens," JJ suggested.

"Eyesore Estates?" Ray asked.

"Twin Silos," Dad said.

Ray snorted, but JJ's laugh stuck in his throat. "You're
kidding."

Even Hampton had been full of dairy farms once, and
Dad had already told them about the silos that still rose in
the middle of the building site. They were the beautiful
old wooden kind.

"They can put spigots at the bottom," Ray said, "and
fill 'em with Perrier water. Or line 'em with tiles for the
world's deepest hot tubs!"

Dad chuckled, but poked at his chicken bones. "That's
prime, fertile land we're building on. It's a sobering sight."

There was too long a silence. After selling the land that
was now Hillcrest Drive, Dad had seemed down for
months. Only open land could keep alive the hope that
someday, somehow, farms would thrive again.

JJ cleared his throat. "Dad," he said, "when can I drive
the corn wagons?"

Dad looked up and smiled again, which was just what
JJ had wanted.

9

Gram came home the next day, and though everyone tried to make her rest, she was all the more defiant: "Give me that peeler. I'm not useless yet!"

Sometimes she faltered on a long word, or let a sentence trail unfinished. Then JJ saw a lost expression slacken her face, and he looked away. By the time he looked back, Gram's lips were pressed firm again, her eyes sharp.

"Just can't take words for granted," she said, and that was all the acknowledgment she gave her stroke.

Still, for the next few days, they tried to do things behind her back—take out the compost, put in a load of laundry—and, as if by chance, someone was always around the house. Mom and Ray kept up the corn harvest by taking turns. Ray stayed near Gram while Mom chopped a wagonful and drove it home; then Mom had a cup of coffee in the kitchen while Ray unloaded. When JJ got home, he did his homework, practiced his clarinet, cleaned his room while Mom and Ray harvested a few loads more efficiently.

On Saturday afternoon, JJ sat at the kitchen table doing math problems. Gram was making bread. At first, she talked to him from time to time—asked about band, told him about a young nurse at the hospital who played the tuba.

JJ smiled. "Now, how'd you find that out, Gram?"

She shrugged. "Just talking."

Then she seemed to disappear into her own thoughts.

Concentrating on his math problems, JJ only half noticed a steady little sound, as if the bread board were squeaking as Gram kneaded the dough. Then Gram coughed, and there was silence for a while before the sound started up again. JJ listened without looking up. *Gram* was making that sound: each breath came out with a short, soft note, like a tiny, staccato whimper: *Awh. Awh. Awh. Awh.*

JJ looked at Gram without turning his head. She was concentrating on her work. Her glasses had slipped down on her nose, and she shoved them up again with the back of her floury hand, but the sound was uninterrupted. *Awh. Awh. Awh.* She didn't seem to hear it.

JJ could hear nothing else. He focused hard on the numbers in front of him, but trying to ignore the sound just made it seem louder.

"Gram?"

"What, dear?" She raised her eyebrows without looking at him.

"Never mind."

There. Silence—just the soft squishing of the dough.

Then the sound came back. Already JJ hated it. *Awh. Awh. Awh. Awh.* He felt as if someone were poking him, forcing him to notice what he wanted to ignore: he had taken Gram for granted—they all had. JJ'd been worrying about doing more farm work, but who would do Gram's work if she got sick? How would the farm keep going then?

Awh. Awh. Awh. It was like the ticking of a clock, slow and steady and relentless, insisting that JJ face the truth: Gram was going to die. Maybe not soon, but someday. It was obvious, of course, but somehow he'd never realized it before. Now her every breath reminded him.

The phone rang and JJ jumped up. "I'll get it."

It was Steven. "Hi, jazz man!"

"Hey." JJ's throat felt tight.

"What're you doing?"

"Nothing much."

"How's your gram?"

"Fine. I mean . . ."

"So, can you come over?"

"Nah, I don't think so."

"Why not?"

"Well . . ." JJ swallowed carefully. He was very aware of Gram in the next room. Her hearing was as good as ever. "It's kind of a busy weekend," he said.

"I thought you just said—"

"Yeah, but I mean, I kind of need to stick around."

"Shoot. Well, anyway, I forgot to tell you I won't be on the bus on Monday—or Tuesday either."

"What's up?"

"Jewish New Year."

"Oh." JJ was pretty sure the Lerners didn't go to stupid parties with hats and blowers, but what *did* they do for two days? "A double holiday," he said. "Pretty good deal." He grinned into the receiver. "I could use one myself."

There was a tiny silence.

"So," Steven said, "you can tell Ms. Byron not to worry." Now he laughed a little. "I'm not sick. I'll be there Wednesday for jazz band."

"Okay." JJ hadn't thought about jazz band. He sure wouldn't be doing *that* now, but he wasn't ready to explain things to Steven.

JJ could hear Mrs. Lerner talking in the background.

"Just a sec," Steven said, and there was the muffling sound of his hand over the mouthpiece. Then he was back. "JJ? Mom says to remind you, she can't give you a ride the Wednesday after next—you know, the fourth."

"Another holiday?"

"Yeah. So your Dad can pick you up, right?"

"Don't worry about it, Steven. I'm probably not doing that anyway."

"Doing what?"

JJ was still aware of Gram. "Staying after school and all."

"You mean for jazz band?"

"Yeah."

"You mean you're thinking of quitting *jazz band*?"

64

Steven's voice had started to change, and now it cracked.

"It's just that I think I'm gonna be too busy."

"Too busy?" Steven laughed. "You're always too busy, J, but you can't quit jazz band—it's like the best thing that's ever happened to us. And, hey, you're the star, man! She won't even do it without you."

The phone felt slimy, and JJ realized his hands were sweating. "There's that sixth-grader—Jennifer—she's getting pretty good."

"I don't believe it. You're serious, aren't you?"

"Yeah. I guess I am."

"You can't do this, JJ. You'll screw up the whole thing. It's only one afternoon a week. Can't Ray do your chores or something?"

"He's doing his, and anyway it's not just chores. It's corn harvest, and—"

"I don't believe this. You're gonna quit jazz band to pick *corn*?"

"We don't pick it, Steven, and besides, it's not just corn, it's the whole farm. I mean . . ." JJ wished he hadn't started all this. He couldn't think clearly. He couldn't explain. Especially not with Gram in the next room. "It's like if I'm not here . . . I don't know. Maybe after corn harvest."

"Oh, right! And then it'll be hay or manure or syrup or something. I don't believe this, JJ!"

"Hey, look. You're the one taking holidays."

"JJ, these are like the biggest—"

"Yeah, so I need some extra holidays, too."

"*Extra* holidays?"

"Well, I mean—"

"You know something, JJ? You're really full of it."

"*I'm* full of it?"

"Yeah. *You're* full of it." And there was a click on the line.

"Steven?"

Silence.

"Steven?"

More clicks, then a loud dial tone.

JJ slammed down the receiver. "Jerk!"

"Jerk?"

Shoot! Gram had heard, of course.

JJ didn't look at her as he went to collect his homework. He just wanted to get outside and do something useful.

"Wasn't that Steven?" Gram asked.

"Yeah."

"You two fighting?"

"He's being weird."

A little mischief came into Gram's voice. "Never bothered you before."

JJ couldn't even smile. "Maybe it did," he said. "Maybe I just never said so."

"Play a little music with him," Gram said. She was spreading a damp dish towel over the bowl of rising dough. "After two or three measures, you'll forget your differences."

JJ slammed his math book shut. "He's a jerk!"

He felt Gram look at him hard, and he glanced at her. "He doesn't have a clue about farms, Gram. I mean, he was talking about syruping after corn harvest!"

"And what does that have to do with music?"

"Lots. The way he acts, you'd think this place was nothing—and I'm nuts, just because some things are more important than jazz band."

"Like what, for instance?"

JJ looked at Gram. Like you, he wanted to say, but Gram was staring him down. She had taken hold of the back of a chair and faced him with her shoulders squared.

He looked down at his homework paper. "I don't know. Everything."

"Look at me, Felix John Jaquith."

Now, why was *she* mad at him?

"Hey," he started, but her look silenced him. Her eyes were fierce, piercing his own double reflection in her glasses.

"You stay in that jazz band," she said.

"Hey, what's the big deal? I just—"

"Steven or no Steven, you stay in that jazz band."

"Okay, Gram! Anything you say!"

Gram's shoulders relaxed, and she turned away. "Growing up on a farm doesn't make you a farmer."

"What's that supposed to mean?"

"You're Felix John Jaquith II," Gram said. "Not Ed, not Ray, not Steven." JJ watched her back as she wiped the counter. "And not Felix John Jaquith I, either. You let this farm start defining you now . . ." She trailed off as if the rest of the sentence were obvious.

"Gram?" JJ said.

She looked around and smiled. "Now, have you grained the heifers today?"

"No, but—"

"Then get on out there and quit hovering, would you?"

"Sure, Gram."

JJ went to take his homework to his room. How had things ended up like this? Now he'd be in jazz band, but he sure wasn't taking any rides from Steven, so he'd have to wait for Dad at Whitcomb's and miss milking altogether. Great. Now Gram would be alone even more. But she'd have kicked him out anyway, so what did it matter?

He stopped halfway down the stairs. It didn't matter. *He* didn't matter. That was the truth of it. If Ray decided to quit, there was nothing JJ could do about it. He couldn't take Ray's place.

By the time he passed back through the kitchen, JJ felt so small he wasn't surprised that Gram didn't notice him. She was reading a cookbook, and with every breath, she made that little sound again: *Awh. Awh. Awh. Awh.*

JJ slipped outside. Gram was getting old, and there was nothing he could do about that, either.

10

The next morning, Dad was home, and JJ actually slept late. He was awakened by the sound of a truck beeping as it backed up. That would be Dick, coming to collect the milk. JJ imagined Mom and Dad knew Dick's last name, but no one ever used it. Dick came every other day, drew off the milk from the bulk tank to the silver truck, filled out a form to say how much he'd taken, chatted for a bit if anyone was around, and headed off to the next farm.

JJ checked the clock. It was only eight. Steven wouldn't be up yet. If JJ decided to call him, he'd have to wait till after breakfast.

JJ got down to the kitchen just as Mom and Dad came in from the barn. They were talking about ordinary things—the calf born during the night, May's next breeding, Gert's sore foot—but JJ recognized the funny glow that seemed to surround them, as if choring together was their idea of romance.

Gram was dressed for church, which reminded JJ that Steven would be going to temple for Sunday school. JJ would call him in the afternoon.

At breakfast, Dad looked around at the family. "Seems to me," he said, "we've got the perfect morning"—he smiled directly at JJ—"for teaching this young man to drive a corn wagon."

"All *right*!" JJ said.

The weather was sunny, warming from the night's light frost toward a high in the seventies. JJ drove Old John out to the cornfield with Mom and Dad riding the fenders. Dad chopped the first load, while Mom and JJ stood watching as if there were endless time. The harvester's spout curved like the arm of a dancer over the wagon, spraying the chopped corn into a golden heap.

Mom spoke to JJ over the noise. "The real danger of this job," she said, "is that it's so monotonous—and so beautiful. It's easy to get hypnotized, forget to pay attention." Even Ray wasn't allowed to drive the chopper yet, but Mom seemed to be thinking about the day when JJ would drive it. "You've got to guide those blades just right—and keep checking the spout, too."

After a few times around the field, Dad stopped the machinery and JJ unhitched the full wagon. Mom switched New John to an empty one and headed off to chop the next load.

"Now," Dad said to JJ, "back Old John right up here."

It took JJ three tries to back the tractor hitch near enough to the wagon hitch.

Finally, Dad could line up the holes and drop in the steel pin. "Great job! Now let that clutch out real easy."

"Aren't you riding?"

Dad smiled. "Not yet."

Slowly, JJ let out the clutch. The gears seemed to engage about where he expected them to, but nothing happened. He let the clutch out a little more. The tractor lurched, so JJ disengaged the clutch, but already the wagon had slammed forward, making the steel pin clang. Dad would have fallen off.

"If you watch the hitch," Dad said, "you'll see it start to pull."

On the fourth or fifth try, JJ got it right, but Dad had to see several smooth starts before he climbed on. "Okay, J. Take us home."

Mom was passing back around with the chopper. JJ waved, but she didn't even glance their way.

The tractor crept slowly toward the road.

"Now, watch out for that ditch there," Dad said. "That's right. Good."

The straight parts were easy, but turns had to be made wide. At the driveway, JJ almost smashed the wagon into the mailbox.

"Wouldn't be the first time that happened," Dad said. "Now back up a little and try again."

Backing up just made things worse. Before long, the tractor was at right angles to the wagon, blocking the road. Then a car came along. Dad took the wheel, turned it a little this way, then that, and eased right up the driveway,

71

waving back at the car. Ray emerged from the house to begin the unloading.

There were three more trips with Dad on the fender before JJ felt he was getting the hang of it.

"Okay, J," Dad said when the next wagon was full. "You're on your own."

"Here goes nothing," JJ said, but he let the clutch out carefully and seemed to glide into motion. It was like making a smooth entrance on his clarinet.

Ray still had to take over to back the wagons into position for unloading, but on the stretch between field and home JJ sat tall on the tractor, the sun strong on his back, the hills aglow with fall color. Alone with the loud churn of Old John, he even dared to sing.

A car passed, with a kid around JJ's age in the back seat. JJ only glanced down, but the kid was looking up at him with such an expression of awe and envy that JJ almost laughed. He wished Steven would drive by. But Steven wouldn't look at him that way. Steven didn't think this work was exciting or impressive. He only saw the time it took—as if *he* wasn't spending half his life in some synagogue.

JJ swung wide as he reached the driveway. He looked back to watch the wagon take the turn. Perfect.

Why did he have to keep thinking about Steven? Steven thought JJ was quitting jazz band. JJ'd definitely have to call him after supper.

He waited till Gram had gone early to bed, Ray had gone off with friends, and Mom and Dad were in the front room conferring about which bills to pay next.

His stomach got tight the minute he picked up the receiver. If only Steven hadn't hung up on him!

The phone rang twice. "Hello."

"Hey, St—" But the voice kept going.

Steven had put a new message on the answering machine: ". . . leave your name and number after the beep."

And then came the beep.

JJ hung up quickly. He'd forgotten about Steven's holiday. This must be New Year's Eve.

It made a lot of sense, actually, starting the year in September. If farmers could choose, they'd start it in spring, when the land thawed and came to life again. But with school opening and the crops all in, fall felt like a real beginning, too. On January 1, nothing was new but calendars.

JJ didn't call again. He figured it might be rude, disturbing the family now. He'd just have to wait till Wednesday and talk to Steven on the bus.

On Wednesday morning, the bus was late. Seven cars and trucks had passed since JJ'd started counting. He stood across the road, his back to the river, and wondered what he'd say to Steven. Sorry? Well, he *had* changed his mind, thanks to Gram, but he'd had good reasons for deciding to quit jazz band. Why should he apologize? Besides, Steven was the one who'd hung up.

Another car. That made eight, and still no bus.

JJ watched Ray come out of the barn to draw some molasses from the tank. Ray would dribble it over the hay to entice the cows to eat the last scraps.

A blue pickup rattled by. Nine. JJ waved automatically, because it was Ham's truck. Where was Ham headed at this time of day? Oh, yeah. Ham wasn't a farmer anymore. He could be going anywhere. JJ watched the pickup clatter up the hill and out of sight. Then the bus was there, looming toward him with lights flashing and the door folding back.

JJ felt his face prepare a smile for Steven. If Steven smiled back, or even looked at him as he came down the aisle, JJ would say "Sorry" as he slid into their seat.

Their seat was empty. Hadn't Steven said two days? Maybe he *had* gotten sick. JJ slid over to the window. He'd definitely call Steven after school.

It wasn't till the next stop, when a whole bunch of kids got on, that JJ noticed the back of Steven's head. He was sitting right near the front on the other side, next to a first-grader. The little kid was talking steadily, but Steven stared right past him out the window.

Jerk!

JJ set his clarinet on the seat next to him. If Steven weren't so busy being a jerk, he'd have noticed the clarinet. He'd know that JJ wasn't quitting.

At lunch, Steven sat at a different table. At recess, he played on the opposite kickball team. In social studies, he somehow ended up in the other discussion group.

Now, when JJ showed up at jazz band, Steven would be the one who'd have to say he was sorry.

Instead, Steven set up the drums by himself, acting as if JJ were invisible. JJ sat down to put his clarinet together.

He played some scales. Once, when he glanced at Steven, Steven was just glancing away, looking disgusted. Maybe he thought JJ'd just been jerking him around, threatening to quit for no reason. Well, how was JJ supposed to explain if Steven wouldn't talk to him?

Ms. Byron got them working on "Memories of You."

"Now, what you're aiming for here, JJ, is a chance to really improvise. The drums are holding things down, so you can take off."

They played the piece through. JJ got every note right, but he sure wasn't going to experiment with Steven there acting superior.

Ms. Byron went over a rough spot with the trumpets. Then she turned to JJ again. "Good job, JJ, but you're playing it too straight. You know the jazz progressions—use some other notes from those chords." She smiled at him. "Let it swing a little."

They played the piece again.

Ms. Byron shrugged. "Okay, folks, let's move on. But, JJ—when you're jamming with Steven, try messing around over the steady beat. You want to loosen up a little."

JJ nodded without moving his eyes from his music stand. He could practice just fine by himself.

He was glad when rehearsal ended. He got out of there fast. Mrs. Lerner was waiting in her car right outside the school. She smiled and waved. JJ nodded and walked on past toward Whitcomb's store.

Mrs. Lerner rolled down her window. "Aren't you riding with us, JJ?"

"No, thanks. My dad's coming."

He hadn't told Dad to stop for him. He'd never imagined Steven would keep this up. Now JJ'd have to call home and tell them he'd be late—too late to help with the milking. He'd have to hang around the store for an hour and then go wave Dad down. Some friend Steven had turned out to be!

By regular band on Friday, it was obvious to Ms. Byron and everyone else that something had changed between JJ and Steven.

That afternoon, Steven didn't even ride the bus. JJ saw him walking with Tommy Marston to Tommy's house. JJ knew for a fact that Tommy thought music was for girls.

Steven was absent for the next jazz-band rehearsal.

"Anybody know what's wrong with Steven?" Ms. Byron asked. She didn't look at JJ, but a few kids automatically glanced his way.

"Holiday," JJ muttered.

"Oh, of course." Ms. Byron seemed embarrassed. "Yom Kippur. Of course. Thanks, JJ."

Without drums, the music sounded hollow. JJ just wanted to get out of there. He'd brought something to read at Whitcomb's, and this time Dad knew to stop for him.

As soon as he'd put his clarinet away, he headed for the door.

"JJ?" Ms. Byron called.

He turned. He'd forgotten to fold his chair. "Oh, sorry," he said, and went back to fold it.

"Got a minute?"

JJ shrugged. "Guess so."

There were still a few kids milling around. " 'Night, Ms. Byron."

"Good night, Mark. Great job today. Now work on that syncopation, okay?"

JJ waited awkwardly.

Finally, they were alone.

Ms. Byron unfolded a couple of chairs and had him sit down facing her.

"So what's up?" she said.

"What d'you mean?"

"Between you and Steven."

JJ shrugged and looked at the clarinet case on his knees. "You'd have to ask him that, I guess."

"I already did."

JJ glanced up. Then he focused on the case again. "So what'd he say?"

"Something about your quitting."

"But I didn't."

"You were thinking of it?"

"Things are kind of busy at home."

"But you worked it out?"

"You could say that."

"Good," Ms. Byron said, and laughed. "Cause you'd've had to fight with *me* to quit."

"With Gram, too."

"So let me get this straight. Why's Steven still mad at you?"

"Good question."

"You sound mad at him."

JJ shifted in his chair. He looked at the clock across the room. "He didn't turn out to be such a great friend, that's all."

Ms. Byron sighed and leaned back in her chair. "It's one thing to be mad at your friend . . ."

Former friend, JJ thought.

". . . but you're letting it mess up your music."

JJ felt stung. "I thought I was playing pretty well," he said.

"Of course you are. But your heart isn't in it."

JJ didn't have an answer for that. It was true. He didn't care that much about jazz band anymore. About any of it. He had more important things on his mind.

Ms. Byron sighed again. "Something's bothering you, JJ, but if you won't talk about it . . ." She trailed off and waited.

JJ tried to think of something to say. Some people—like Liz, or Lindy—seemed to have words for everything: *I feel this,* or *you seem that.* JJ wished he could make Ms. Byron understand, but what was he supposed to tell her—how hard it was to back up a tractor with a wagon hitched to it? That's what it felt like, trying to straighten things out at home.

"JJ," Ms. Byron said, "when you're going through rough times, the music can help."

She seemed to speak from experience, and JJ looked at her, suddenly wondering what rough times she'd had.

She smiled. "The music can help," she said again.

JJ looked away. She sure hadn't been through rough times on a farm. How could music help to get the crops in?

"Sorry," he said. "I'm doing the best I can."

Ms. Byron sighed and stood up. "Well, I hope you and Steven can patch things up."

This time JJ remembered to fold his chair, but he could hardly wait to get outside. The cold air felt great on his face. There was a three-day weekend coming up for Columbus Day, and the fall colors would be at their peak. The farm would get a lot of maple-syrup customers, and families would stop in just to show the calves to kids who'd never seen one.

11

Fall blazed forth across the hillsides, setting the maples aflame, then died back suddenly to embers—oak trees glowing deep orange in the slanting sun. By the end of October, the corn harvest was finished—not so very late, after all.

JJ and Steven didn't patch things up. They just got used to not being friends. They could sit at the same lunch table or work in the same discussion group. It was no big deal. JJ explained to anyone who asked that Steven was buddies with Tommy Marston these days. Which was fine with JJ. Now he could be a farm kid without anybody hassling him.

The nights were already cold enough to keep the milkers in. For such galumphing beasts, cows were strangely delicate once they started giving milk. Any stress to their systems could make them sick, or at least reduce their production.

Now all the work focused on the coming winter. The empty heifer barn had to be readied—broken stanchions repaired, new leaks in the rusty water system fixed. The windows in the milk barn were installed again, and the milk-room windows were covered with plastic, creating the warm foggy feeling that felt like winter to JJ. But it wasn't real winter till they brought the heifers in, and Dad didn't believe in cooping up animals until absolutely necessary.

This year, "absolutely necessary" came early. In the middle of November, there was a sudden cold snap. Snow and freezing rain were predicted. Dad was home on Saturdays now, but Saturday might be too late. "Today," Mom announced during the Friday-morning milking, "the heifers come home."

JJ was just leaving the barn to change for school. "Save the bred heifers for last," he said. "I want to be there to bring Claire in."

Sketch seemed to have decided for herself that the time had come. She circled restlessly. Today she'd be needed more than ever. She'd round up each group—the older calves, the yearlings, the bred heifers—and bring them to the roadside gate, then hold them steady for hours while they were led into the truck, a few at a time, and taken home.

JJ felt as restless as Sketch. Winter had arrived. The farm would suddenly be smaller and closer, a huddle of steamy buildings in the wide expanse of frozen land that waited till spring.

"I wish I could skip school," he remarked to Gram.

"I thought you had band today," she said.

"Yeah, well . . ." Gram was looking closely at him, and he didn't go on. Except for little hesitations in her speech and that tiny sound she made unawares, Gram seemed as strong as ever.

Regular band—concert band, as Ms. Byron now called it—had gotten boring.

At least Ms. Byron didn't bug him anymore. In his individual lessons, she cheered whenever he played a few unwritten notes, but around other kids, she just smiled at him patiently. She seemed to be waiting for something, but he couldn't imagine what.

"Steven," she was saying now. "The bells have to be pianissimo by measure 54. So start toning it down way back at 43."

Ms. Byron was gearing up for the winter concert. They were working on "Jingle Bells." JJ's part was so simple he hadn't even practiced it. At least in jazz band they were doing "Jingle Bell Rock."

JJ looked at the clock. He tried to guess how many heifers were back in the barn by now. He'd meant to remind Ray to save the end stall for Claire. That way, she'd be the first to get her grain, and the last to feel the drafts from the doorway.

"JJ? Are you with us?" Ms. Byron smiled patiently.

When at last JJ got off the school bus and headed up the drive, Sketch came down from the back porch and

stretched as if she'd been sleeping. Why wasn't she working? There was sleet coming down already.

Ray's pickup drove in, and Ray jumped out.

"Hey, Squirt!"

He was wearing a good jacket, new jeans, and his fancy
cowboy boots. Had he been on a date? His hair was
combed, and he was beaming.

"What happened to the heifers?" JJ asked. "I thought
we were bringing them home."

"*We* already have. Got the calves and yearlings in easy.
Mom said you wanted to help with Claire's lot."

"Yeah, but— Where've *you* been?"

"Well, since you asked so nicely, Squirt"—Ray leaned
back lazily against his truck—"I've been at a job interview."

"*Job* interview! What *kind* of job?"

"Well, this one was for the fertilizer plant—truck driver, basically, but—"

"Ray, you can't do that!" JJ was just standing there in
the sleet, holding the mail and his clarinet.

"On the contrary," Ray said. "They already offered me
the job." JJ felt punched in the stomach, but Ray didn't
even pause. "I turned it down, though. I'm hoping for
something closer to Hampton. Got a new girlfriend—"

"Ray, you can't do this."

"That's what *I* thought. No degree. No skills. But driving trucks, fixing 'em—some people think that's worth
something." Ray went around to the passenger side of the
truck to take out a bag of groceries. He was in such high
spirits he was practically dancing.

JJ was glad his hands were full. He felt like slapping that grin. "And what are the rest of us supposed to do?"

"Aw, come on, Squirt, you know Mom and Dad. They'll muddle through. They always have."

Ray was heading for the house and JJ felt pulled along behind him. The sleet was coming down harder.

"You have to wait, Ray. You have to stay till I—"

Ray turned sharply on the steps to the porch. "No, JJ. I'm not staying." Then he paused. He looked down at JJ and at the clarinet in his hand. "And from the looks of things, kid, neither are you."

"What's *that* supposed to mean?"

Ray had gone on into the dimness. He stopped to pry off his boots without sitting down. "You wait, Squirt. You won't stay either. Music school, maybe? But believe me: you and that clarinet are already headed out of here."

JJ set down the clarinet as if it had burned him. "You got that wrong. I'm quitting." He heard himself say it before he'd even thought it.

"Yeah, right!" Ray said. "I'll believe *that* when I see it!"

Before JJ could duck away, Ray reached out and tousled his hair, then took the groceries in to Gram. "Meet you in fifteen to go get those last heifers," he called as the door closed behind him.

The clarinet case had beads of water on it. JJ wiped it with his sleeve and sat down to open it. He stared at the smooth black wood nested in maroon velvet. What once had seemed dark and magical now seemed dark and threatening. He had said the truth without knowing it: he was going to quit. Gram was the one who'd made him keep going, and it was time he stood up to her anyway. He'd do the winter concert for Ms. Byron, and then he'd quit for good.

Steven probably wouldn't even notice.

12

Just as December arrived, the snow came in earnest: a big storm, then a little storm. With snow wrapped around the barnyard thick and heavy, everything inside the plowed clearing seemed snug. The barn seemed warmer, the kitchen steamier, the family closer.

Then, on the first Wednesday of the month, there was another big storm. It knocked out the electricity. School was cancelled for the second time, and Dad didn't even try to get into Hampton. They did the morning milking by hooking up the vacuum pump to the power takeoff on the biggest tractor. In the gray light of the kitchen, Gram congratulated herself for keeping the old gas stove, and served them muffins by candlelight. Later, only a few hours behind schedule, Dick showed up in his silver tank truck to take away the milk. Even in winter, he wore his shirt open at the neck, exposing a wide V of bare chest.

It was just a week later that JJ awoke to the muffled

sounds of the tractor moving forward and back, forward and back. It must have snowed again in the night. He looked out the window. The floodlight was on in the yard. Ray had nearly finished the plowing, and Mom was shoveling the path to the milkhouse. The snow had stopped, leaving three or four more inches. If school was cancelled again, they'd miss another jazz-band rehearsal. Ms. Byron was getting worried about the winter concert—only a week and a day away.

JJ's stomach tightened. Would he really be able to quit after that? He remembered the way Ray had laughed. *I'll believe it when I see it.* JJ set his jaw.

When he got down to the kitchen, the radio was on. Dad was just finishing his breakfast.

"Well, good morning," he said cheerfully. "You just missed the school announcements—two-hour delay."

"Hardly seems worth it," Gram said, "starting school so late."

"Yeah," JJ said, "but it's Wednesday. Ms. Byron'll get her rehearsal."

"*Her* rehearsal?" Gram asked, but Dad was still talking about the delay.

"Farmer's hours," he said, and winked at JJ. "You can chore and wash up, have a leisurely breakfast, and still have to wait for that bus." He stood up to clear his plate. "See you at Whitcomb's?" He clapped JJ on the shoulder before he left.

Ray was off all morning, plowing driveways. Maybe, with that business booming this winter, Ray would put off looking for a job.

JJ helped Mom with the milking, and when it was almost done, he went out back to shovel the snow from the long wooden feed trough in the yard. The sun had come up bright and convincing, so the school delay seemed silly, but he wasn't complaining. He went to start the silo unloader, and as the corn tumbled down onto the rumbling conveyor, he helped Mom turn the cows out. The conveyor carried the silage out over the feed trough, showering it onto the cows' lowered heads. May stopped eating to lift her face and sniff at the raining feed.

"Like me and my coffee," Mom said. "Let's go eat."

Even after breakfast, JJ had an hour before he'd have to get ready for school. He and Mom cleaned the barn. The wide gutter in the floor along the stalls collected most of the manure, and at the throw of a switch, iron paddles slowly pushed the manure toward a scuttle hole, where it fell onto the pile under the barn. In spring the manure would be used as fertilizer, spread by the wagonload across the fields. "The original recycling," Dad called it.

Mom took a wheelbarrow to go shovel out the calf pens. JJ hoed the manure from the stalls into the gutter. When the iron paddles finished their job, he pushed the heavy paper shredder into the center alley. Donning ear protectors, he started the machine and began feeding bags of newspaper into its loud, revolving maw. This was his favorite part of cleaning the barn, and he didn't get to do it very often. The shredded paper served as bedding for the cows, and soaked up moisture in the gutter. As it spilled out of the machine, JJ raked it down the alley into a long, fluffy pile, then sent it flying into the stalls and tumbling into the gutter. The sun shone almost horizontal across the floor, making the fluttering paper seem to sparkle. For a moment, before the cows came back in, the barn would look white and clean as if new snow had fallen here, too. The ear protectors gave it all a faraway feeling, and JJ half danced through the work, humming to himself, then even singing.

He stopped abruptly when a shadow blinked across the sunlight. Someone had used the door by the grain bin and come in along the windows: a woman in a green coat, leather boots. Odd time for a syrup customer. Had he been dancing when this lady came in?

Then the woman stepped out of the light behind her, and JJ recognized Mrs. Lerner. Her face looked worried or scared, and JJ's stomach flipped. Had something happened to Steven? Mrs. Lerner looked around, as if trying to figure out how to move closer, but she could hardly climb through the stanchions in those clothes. She spoke from where she was, but JJ couldn't hear her and he realized he'd been standing there, gaping, with the ear protectors still on. He yanked at them and sprang to turn off the machine.

". . . all right?" Mrs. Lerner was shouting into the sudden silence.

"What?" JJ said, confused.

"The cows," Mrs. Lerner said, and waved a gloved hand toward the windows. "They're—"

Mom was just rumbling in with a wheelbarrow heaped with soggy, reeking bedding from the calf pens.

"What's up, J?" she said, and then saw Mrs. Lerner. "Oh. Hello." She set down the wheelbarrow and came forward. "How are you?" Mom laughed a little. "You'll forgive me if I don't shake your hand."

"I was headed for work," Mrs. Lerner said, "and saw your cows in the road, so—"

"What?" JJ ran to slide open the back door. The barnyard was empty. A section of wire was down. He looked out toward the road, and there, lumbering ridiculously through the snow, was sore-footed Gert, trying to catch up to the others.

Mom had come up behind him. "Holy Hannah!" she said. "Where's Sketch? Sketch!"

Sketch came running from the warm milk house, and Mom followed her out across the snow. "Get some grain!" she called to JJ.

JJ grabbed an empty bucket.

"Excuse me," he said, because Mrs. Lerner was right beside the grain cart.

"Anything I can do?" she asked.

"No," JJ said, scooping up grain and slapping it into the pail. "But, I mean, thanks."

"JJ?"

He glanced at her as he emptied the scoop. Three should do it.

Mrs. Lerner had paused in the doorway. "I think Steven would like to—"

"Excuse me," JJ said again, heading outside. By running along the road, he could catch up to Mom. "Thanks again," he called back to Mrs. Lerner, "and hi to—" What was he saying? And what had Mrs. Lerner just said?

Later for that. Now he could see along the road to where the cows were crossing it and stumbling down the bank toward the river.

Mom had been slowed by the deep snow. "Fools!" she shouted to the cows. Jet was in the lead, already crossing in the shallows. "That Jet," Mom said as she and JJ met on the road, "has lots of personality, all of it negative. And if she breaks a leg . . ." Mom didn't complete the threat. The other cows were hesitating at the water's edge. "Maybe they have a *little* sense," Mom said.

She sent Sketch to circle wide and bring Jet in. JJ stood on the road and shook the grain to lure the others back up the bank.

"Come, boss!" he boomed, and soon all but Jet had joined ranks behind him.

They'd already strained themselves enough by coming across the field in the snow. He'd have to lead them along the road, up the drive, and into the barn from the front. He needed to run ahead to open the big overhead door and move the paper shredder out of the alley.

He looked over his shoulder to see if Sketch was available to help him, but then he heard a car coming. He moved back alongside the cows, flapping his arms and swinging the bucket to shoo them over. As the car passed, he realized that there was another vehicle waiting to get by from the other side. It was the school bus. Suddenly JJ became aware of the manure on his jacket and the bits of newspaper that were probably clinging to his wool cap. He didn't look up at the bus windows, but he could feel faces staring and grinning. One of those faces would be Steven's. What had Mrs. Lerner tried to say?

As the bus eased by, the driver opened her window. "Sorry," she said.

Now the cows noticed the barn and veered off the road into the snow, as eager to get home as if they'd been forced to leave.

"Hey!" JJ yelled.

This was nuts. Even if no cow broke a leg, they'd all give less milk. JJ took off after them, but there was a crust under the new snow, and it held JJ's weight only until he lifted the other foot. He kept sinking through up to his knees, lumbering as awkwardly as the cows. He had to stop and catch his breath.

Then Sketch sped by, skimming through the fresh powder.

JJ laughed. "Unfair advantage," he called back to Mom.

Jet had insisted on crossing the snow, too, and Mom was bringing up the rear, just in case. Sketch was corraling the others now, so JJ waited for Mom.

"What a morning!" she called, laughing. "This'll shorten the milk tank a bit!"

With each step, she was lifting her knee practically to her chin, then pitching forward to get some distance. She wasn't wearing a hat, and her hair was bobbing wildly into her face. She saw JJ watching her and added a flapping motion with her arms. JJ started laughing, and Mom laughed, too, and JJ laughed harder. Now the whole morning seemed hysterically funny, especially when, in the middle of a lurching step, Mom sat down abruptly in the snow. "Oof!"

JJ half expected her to lie back and make a snow angel. But then Sketch barked sharply, and he turned to see that Jet was heading up the slope toward the cider-apple trees.

By the time JJ had slogged ahead and flailed his arms at Jet to turn her around, Sketch had all the others back in the yard and was lying at the break in the fence, staring them down.

Why hadn't Mom fixed the fence?

She was still sitting back there in the snow, and JJ grinned in confusion. "Mom?"

Her smile looked strained. "Soon as you get that fence up, I need some help here."

"What's the matter?" JJ ran to her, cursing the hobbling snow.

"My knee," she said. When she tried to adjust her position, pain shot across her face. She lay back. "Go fix that fence," she said. "Then bring your old sled." She smiled up at him. "Believe me, I'll still be here."

When JJ got Mom to the porch steps, she sat on the bottom one with the injured knee stretched out, then hoisted herself up one step at a time. Now JJ realized that the leg she'd straightened was her right one. "But that's your *good* knee," he said.

"Not anymore."

Ray drove in, jumped out, and came running.

"Good," Mom said to him before she explained a thing. "You can run JJ over to school, leave a note for the breeder and the supply truck, and then I think I'll have the doctor look at this."

When JJ finally got to school, it was close to dismissal time. He didn't stay for jazz band. He'd be needed at home, and anyway, in all the confusion, he'd forgotten his clarinet.

13

JJ and Ray were almost finished with the milking that night when the phone rang. The sound seemed to jolt JJ's memory, and he knew it would be Dad.

"Oh, shoot! I forgot about Whitcomb's." JJ climbed through the stanchions to grab the phone on the second ring. "Jaquiths."

"JJ?" In just those two syllables, Dad's voice went from worried to angry.

"Yeah. Hi, Dad. I'm sorry! It's—"

"I told you to leave a message if your band got cancelled."

"Yeah, but Dad—"

"I've already—"

JJ spoke right over him. "Mom hurt her knee, Dad."

There was a silence that seemed to last a long time. "How bad?" Dad said, in a voice too calm.

"The doctor says torn cartilage. She doesn't think

Mom'll need surgery. Just ice and rest. But she wants to look at it again in a few days. We're doing fine, Dad. The milking's almost done."

"Good. I'll be there in fifteen minutes."

When Dad's pickup pulled in, JJ was in the milk house, and through the fog of the plastic, he watched Dad's form hesitate in the driveway, then move toward the barn.

Dad came, grim-faced, through the milk-house door and immediately started to help set up the wash cycle. Ray had gone to feed the calves, and now came back with the empty bucket and bottle.

"Hi," he said to Dad, and Dad just nodded.

Together the three of them headed toward the house, and as they sat on the porch to remove their work boots, JJ heard Dad take a deep breath and force out the air as if getting rid of something. Then Dad stood up and clapped JJ on the shoulder. "Something sure smells good!" he said.

When Dad opened the door to the kitchen, Gram turned at the sink, but said nothing. Mom was at the table with her leg up on a cushioned chair and an ice pack on her knee. Her crutches were parked beside her. Dad stopped in the doorway, and as JJ pushed past, he saw Mom catch Dad's eye with a deep, desperate look. Then she shrugged and smiled thinly.

"Well," Dad said cheerfully, "guess I'll be staying home for a bit." He came into the room and leaned over to kiss Mom as if he always greeted her that way. Then he stood and grinned at everyone. "And you all know how staying home just breaks my heart."

At supper, Ray sat hunched over his food, silent and scowling, but everyone ignored him.

"Dr. Chandrin said to elevate it," Mom said, "above my heart." She laughed. "Now, can't you just see me lying around all day! At least sitting up, I can make myself useful. I'll get the herd records caught up, pay the bills."

Ray looked up then. "With what?" he said.

Mom and Dad glanced at each other and then looked down at their food.

JJ felt like kicking Ray under the table. Everybody knew what this meant. They couldn't do without Dad's income for long. But they'd manage somehow. They'd have to.

It was Gram who broke the silence. "There's plenty more of everything," she said.

"Great!" JJ jumped up to serve himself seconds. He wasn't really hungry, but he didn't want to sit there sulking like Ray.

"Look," Ray said as JJ sat down again. "I think we ought to call Liz. She can come home early."

"She's got exams," Mom said. "She can't miss those."

Ray plunked his fork down hard on his plate. "And why the hell not?"

"Raymond Jaquith," Gram said. "Save your curses for the barn."

Ray pushed his chair back with a loud scrape. "Well, what is so damn— Excuse me. What is so *damned* sacred about Liz and her blasted exams? I can miss my whole *life,* and nobody minds, but—"

"Listen, Ray!" Dad said, and JJ saw him swallow to calm

himself. "Liz got herself a full scholarship, if you'll re-member. That's like money in the bank, but she's still got to earn it. Now, leave her out of this."

"Yeah, well leave me out, too," Ray said, and stood up. Then he added with exaggerated politeness, "Excuse me, Gram."

Slowly and deliberately, he cleared his place, then strode out the door and closed it so carefully that the only sound made was the click of the latch.

A few minutes later, they heard his pickup spin its wheels in the snow before it took off down the driveway.

JJ cleared his place without eating another bite.

"I'm exhausted," Mom said. "I'm going to bed."

She leaned down to pick up her crutches, but Dad stood up. "You're not doing those steep stairs on crutches," he said, and carefully lifted Mom into his arms.

JJ saw her wince with pain, but then she laughed and circled her arms around Dad's neck. "Your blushing bride," she said as they left the room.

That night, JJ couldn't sleep. Even if Mom didn't need surgery, the doctor had said it would be weeks before she could drive a car, let alone work the stiff pedals on a trac-tor. Milking—all those deep knee bends—would be out of the question for months.

JJ rolled over. He went through every detail of the day, trying to understand how things could change so sud-denly—and so completely. His mind kept returning to the smell of the grain in the cart and Mrs. Lerner standing there. *Steven would like to . . .* That's what she said. JJ could hear her clearly now. Why hadn't he let her finish?

JJ stared at the ceiling. He had to admit it: he missed Steven. He could use a friend right now. But it was lucky they hadn't patched things up. Steven would just get angry again—because now JJ really did have to quit the clarinet. Even Gram would see that.

He closed his eyes, determined to keep them closed. He even started to drift off. Then an image floated dreamlike into his vision: Mom like Ernie Adams, hobbling out to the barn with a walker, deformed by the splay of her useless knees.

JJ sat up. He peered at his clock. It was nearly midnight, and he was planning to get up even earlier than usual. He'd set his alarm for 5:30. Ray hadn't come home yet. He'd probably gone into Hampton to see Eileen. He'd never even brought this new girlfriend to the farm, and JJ had a feeling he was trying to make a separate life. Maybe he'd actually stay away. The jerk, taking off when he was needed most.

Mom and Dad were still awake. JJ could hear the rise and fall of voices in their room, but he couldn't distinguish a single word. He slithered back under the covers and put his pillow over his head. That only muffled the sound.

Then there was silence. He put the pillow aside, lifting his head to listen. The silence lasted and his neck got stiff. He rolled over to go to sleep at last, but he thought he heard his parents again.

Yes. There. But this was a different sound, and though

he'd never heard it before, he knew right away what it was: Mom was crying. He'd seen tears in Mom's eyes plenty of times—even just for a calf being born—but now she was sobbing.

JJ felt sick to his stomach.

When he'd been little and come crying to Mom, she'd listened and maybe hugged him, but then she'd ruffled his hair. "Okay, JJ," she'd said, dismissing him. "It's not the end of the world."

"It's not the end of the world," JJ whispered to the ceiling.

But then again, what if it was?

14

The next morning, Mom stayed in bed. Ray had come home—JJ'd checked for his pickup in the dark yard—but as JJ put on his own barn boots, he saw Ray's there on the floor beside Mom's. Ray was still in bed, too.

When JJ stepped out into the cold, he was suddenly afraid to get to the barn. What if Dad came right out with bad news? That this was the last straw. That they were selling the herd. JJ drew in his shoulders and looked up at the looming silhouette of the silos. Up there was that feed sign, the ear of corn with wings. He didn't care how silly he felt. He needed a guardian angel right now. He strained to see it, but the darkness was still too thick.

He was almost at the barn when a pickup pulled into the driveway, blinding him with its headlights. He stood aside as it passed him, glinting blue in the light from the barn. Ham.

JJ waited for him to park and climb out.

"Hi there, son. Your dad in the barn?" Ham stretched to unkink his back.

News traveled fast among farmers. Who had passed it to Ham? The breeder who'd been by yesterday? The supply man?

When Dad looked up from the grain cart, he smiled and adjusted his engineer's cap. "Well, hello there, Ham. You're up early for a man of leisure."

"I was going trout fishing," Ham said, and winked at JJ to be sure he caught the joke, "but you know, if it weren't for bad luck, some people'd have no luck at all. Couldn't find any worms." He chuckled. "Any chance you'd let me milk a bit for old times' sake?"

Dad looked him straight in the eye. "You don't have to do this, Ham."

"Nope," Ham said, and pulled his cap down over his brow, "but I was hoping you'd let me anyhow." Ivory stretched her muzzle toward him, and he patted her neck roughly. "It's getting to seem like a privilege," he said, "just being in a barn."

Dad took a long, deep breath. "I know what you mean," he said.

And that was that. Dad went to work the next day, and Ham just showed up for milking. Soon school would let out for Christmas and Liz would come home. Then the family would manage again.

JJ didn't hear any mention of wages, and doubted Ham would take money anyway. JJ figured Gram would try to pay Ham in pie. That afternoon, when JJ came in from the school bus, Ham was at the kitchen table, swapping stories with Mom and Gram. Their faces turned toward him, still flushed with recent laughter and hot tea.

"My granddaughter says hello," Ham said, and JJ asked how Lindy was doing.

"Got a boyfriend, I guess." Ham winked at Gram. "And she watches a lot of TV."

On Monday afternoon, Lindy was there at the table. JJ almost didn't recognize her. Her hair was pulled back into a perfect, tight knot, and she was wearing silver earrings. If she had on any makeup, it wasn't that obvious. She just looked grown up.

JJ'd had a lesson that day and was carrying his clarinet. He had to sidle behind Lindy's chair to go set it on the piano. She smelled like Mom's hand lotion.

When he got back and stood awkwardly in the door-way, Lindy turned to him. "I came straight from school," she explained. "Grandpa got the bus to drop me here."

JJ didn't know what to say. He felt like a little kid.

Gram handed him a plate. "Sit down and have some pie," she said, and JJ sat down.

Ham was finishing a story, but Lindy spoke to JJ. "How's Claire?"

JJ smiled. "Big."

"Can I see her?"

JJ glanced at Lindy's white sweater. "Now?"

"Sure! I can borrow some barn boots, right? And maybe an old jacket?"

"We've got plenty." JJ shoveled in a huge last bite of pie. He stood up and cleared his plate. "I'll be down in a sec," he said with his mouth full.

As JJ and Lindy crossed the field to the heifer barn, the darkness was already gathering. JJ'd left Sketch whining on the porch. She was a nuisance when she had no work to do.

They had to go single-file on the narrow path of packed snow. JJ took the lead, and they barely spoke. The air was sharply cold, and it must have been the crunch and squeak of their boots that alerted the heifers to their approach. A sudden bawling erupted from inside the heifer barn.

Lindy laughed. "Starving 'em?"

"You bet."

JJ smiled. In just that small exchange, he and Lindy were friends again. She might be a girl and in high school, but on the farm they understood each other. He couldn't explain it any better than that. And he didn't need to.

Inside the barn, he flicked on the light and went straight to Claire. The bawling subsided as the heifers shifted to look over their shoulders at the visitor.

"Oh, come on," JJ said to them all. "It's just Lindy."

Lindy had stopped by the door. He looked back at her. She breathed deeply, and then, without warning, tears streamed down her face. "Oh, shoot!" she said, swiping at them. "Maybe I shouldn't've done this. I mean, just the smell . . ."

"You want to go back?"

"Nah." Lindy laughed in the middle of crying. "I *want* to torture myself."

JJ turned away. "Here's Claire," he said weakly. "I'll go spread some hay."

When that job was done, the only sound in the barn was the peaceful swishing and munching as the animals nuzzled the hay, chose just the right mouthful, and chewed deliberately. As JJ came back around to the alley, he saw that Lindy had buried her face in Claire's neck. He went toward her, but stood on the other side of Claire.

"Are you okay?"

Lindy looked up at him. There were tear tracks under her eyes and across one cheek, but she smiled. "Sorry, J," she said. "Guess I just needed a good cry." She ran a hand the length of Claire's back. "But, yeah, I'm okay." She patted Claire firmly. "Don't have a clue who I *am* anymore— but I guess I'm still okay."

She stepped back into the alley. "You know, J, that's a fine, fancy heifer you've got there."

"Thanks," he said.

This time, Lindy took the lead across the field. The darkness had come and the lights were already on in the milk barn. Ham and Ray were starting the chores.

"I have a feeling," Lindy said over her shoulder, "that now that you've let Grandpa into your barn, you may have trouble getting him out!"

"He's welcome anytime," JJ said. Then he added, "So are you."

"Thanks, J," Lindy said. "You're a good friend, you know that?"

JJ was glad she didn't turn around. It made it easier to say, "You, too."

That was all. JJ knew that when he got to high school and saw Lindy in the halls, they wouldn't have a thing to say to each other, but they *were* good friends in some way. They shared what he and Steven could never share—a whole way of looking at the world.

JJ stopped to fill his lungs with cold air. Lindy crunched on ahead, and silence gathered. He looked at the stars. They always seemed closer in the cold. Ever since Mom's injury, something had changed for JJ. Some realization had been forming in his mind, and now, seeing Lindy, he knew what it was: the farm was more important to him than anything else on earth. He'd known it all along, but suddenly, like the stars, it was sharp and clear and close. It was as if he'd been holding tight to two ropes that pulled him in opposite directions—farming this way, music that way. Even when he'd decided to quit clarinet, music had still tugged at him. He'd felt resentful of Ray, of Steven, even of Ms. Byron. Now, really and truly, he had let go. The whirl of mixed-up feelings—wanting to be older, wanting Ray to hang on, wanting Steven to understand—had all blended into one deep, simple sadness. He had missed Steven terribly, and now he would lose him for good. But it could not be helped. He would give up anything if he could only keep the ground under his feet.

"JJ?" It was Lindy. "Are you okay?"

JJ gulped cold air, then slowly, slowly pushed it out. "Yeah," he said, and meant it. "I'm fine."

15

The day of the winter concert, Liz came home. She was waiting by the mailbox when the school bus pulled up. Her hair was as short as Mom's now, just as curly, and dark the way Mom's used to be. Sometimes it still startled JJ that Mom's hair was gray.

He stepped off the bus into Liz's bear hug.

"You keep *growing*, Squirt!"

JJ didn't care if kids were watching. As the bus roared away, he hugged Liz hard. "Welcome home," he said. He'd forgotten the crisp smell that always clung to his sister—sort of like tart apples. "My concert's tonight," he said as they walked up the drive.

Liz laughed. "Why do you think I skipped out early?"

"You skipped exams?"

"Nah. Just the big end-of-exams-Christmas-Hanukkah-solstice bash."

"Hanukkah?"

"Yeah, it's this week, right? Doesn't Steven celebrate it?"

"I guess so, yeah."

"I can hardly wait till chores," Liz said. "The first year of vet school's all books and no animals. I mean, look." She held out her hands and turned them palms up. "They're getting downright prissy."

"You can take my place," JJ said. "I'm due back at school by 6:30."

When Ray dropped JJ at school, Mrs. Lerner was just dropping Steven. She waved at JJ, and he nodded to her. Several kids were crowding in at once, but JJ waited and held the door for Steven.

"Thanks," Steven muttered as he passed.

"Yeah, and hey, happy Hanukkah."

Steven turned, looking as if he thought this was some kind of joke. Then he shrugged. "Sure," he said. "Thanks." And he went ahead down the hall.

The regular band would play first, then the jazz band, then both together for the grand finale. Ms. Byron used the hour before the concert to go over a few rough spots and rehearse all the seat changes.

JJ found himself watching Steven. He wished he could walk over there and explain everything—about the farm, about quitting. He even imagined Steven slapping him on the back and saying, That's okay, we can still be friends again. But how would they be friends without music?

Some parents had stayed when they brought their kids, and now others were filtering in. Ms. Byron went to stand on the sidelines and wait for her entrance. The cafeteria was nearly full before JJ spotted Dad's engineer's cap. Dad took it off as he came through the door. He was smiling and nodding and saying "Excuse me" to clear a path for Mom on her crutches. Ray and Liz escorted Gram. JJ saw Ms. Byron notice Mom. Did she have a clue what those crutches meant? Would she still blame him for quitting?

Finally, the audience had settled, the principal had welcomed them, and Ms. Byron had come in, bowed, and turned to face the band.

She used a baton for concert band, and now she held it poised. Someone blew a nervous note on a flute. Ms. Byron just smiled and waited. She beat a measure, then another as she mouthed the words: One, two, ready, *play*.

The first piece was a march, all brass and drums at first, but when the clarinets came in, smooth and rich, the sound went through JJ like a slow jolt of electricity. This was the last time. It wasn't just the people he was leaving— it was the music. Every note he played left him as a loss.

He was playing well. He could tell that Ms. Byron knew it, but he didn't dare look at her. With every number and every round of applause, the losses grew and the sadness swelled until JJ could feel pressure at his throat.

Now the jazz band was playing. The group was smaller; Steven was nearer. Ms. Byron conducted from the piano. When JJ looked over for his cue, she caught his eye, smiled, and put one thumb up. JJ swallowed hard.

Then came the finger-snapping beat: "One," *snap,* "two," *snap,* "one, two, three, four."

"Jingle Bell Rock" took off, carrying JJ too fast to the ending, where the drums came in on the upbeat, answered by his solo clarinet.

"BahDAH!"

"WHEEE, dah doodle, ah."

"BahDAH!"

"WHEEE, dah doodle, ah."

JJ and Steven were talking. JJ wanted to say more, wail back at those drums and make them respond, but the pressure in his throat had climbed to sting the back of his eyes, and he was afraid he would cry in front of everyone.

"BahDAH!"

He stared hard at the page and played the written notes. *"WHEEE, dah doodle, ah—daaah."* He let the music end.

As the audience applauded, JJ looked down and squeezed his eyes shut. He didn't dare open them, but neither did he dare keep them closed. Then, as he focused, he saw Gram. She wasn't clapping, just smiling back at him. He had to look away.

When Ms. Byron made him stand along with Steven for a bow, he willed every muscle to tighten against tears. It was over. There was the finale yet to go, but this was the end for JJ. Now he wished he'd hung on to that last piece, taken off with the variations he'd heard in his head. Too late. It was over.

After the finale, there was nothing to do but pack up. JJ sat apart from the bustle. He twisted off the bell of the clarinet and rubbed his thumb along the smooth curve before he nested it in the dark velvet. It was the key joints that gave off that smell of metal and cork grease. He could see the exact placement of his fingers by the spot worn shiny on each key.

Someone passed behind him. "Hey, not bad, JJ."

"Thanks," he muttered.

The barrel next, then— JJ looked up. That had been Steven's voice. But now Steven was sidling into the storage closet with the big bass drum.

Ms. Byron came over. "Great job, JJ. Tonight your heart was in it." She laughed. "For a minute there, I thought you were even going to improvise." She gave his shoulder a little slap. "You'll be swinging soon, JJ. Just keep at it." Then she moved on to congratulate a flutist.

JJ put the mouthpiece away and fiddled with all the pieces until he saw Steven head back toward the drums.

"Hey, you want any help?" he asked.

"No, thanks." But then Steven turned. "I saw your mom. Is she okay?"

"Yeah. I mean, she will be. It's her knee."

"Sorry. I mean, I didn't—" Steven took a deep breath. "Hey. You around over the vacation? You want to jam again?"

JJ looked down and closed the clarinet case. "I wish I could," he said, "but—"

"Sure," Steven said, and headed back to his drums.

The next day was the solstice, the shortest day of the year. School let out for vacation.

That evening after supper, when everyone thought he

111

had gone up to bed, JJ took the clarinet to the attic. Gramp's old tuxedo jacket was spread out carelessly over the boxes. When had JJ left it like that? It had gathered dust. He shook it, then slipped it on. It was still too big, of course. Gramp had been a bigger man than JJ'd ever be.

JJ folded the tuxedo and laid it in its box.

No.

He took it out again, laid the clarinet in the box, and put the tuxedo over it.

When he went down the attic stairs, he didn't even feel like looking back. The darkest day was over.

16

On Christmas Eve, it snowed just enough to cover everything in sparkling white. The farm looked clean and magical, like the farms on Christmas cards. Mom had been hobbling around the house on her crutches, setting out delicate ornaments that JJ vaguely remembered from when he was little.

After supper, Dad actually sat at the old upright piano and started banging out carols. Liz stood behind him to sing, and then Mom joined in, and Ray. "Joy to the world!" they bellowed.

"Hey, JJ," Liz said. "You, too."

By the time they sang all the familiar tunes, Gram had come in from the kitchen and settled in the big chair. In the silence between songs, JJ could hear her breathing: *Awh. Awh. Awh.*

Then they got silly, singing deep-chested like opera

singers as they messed up on "O Holy Night." JJ was just throwing his head back to hit a high note when he noticed his clarinet, sitting right there in its old place on top of the piano. He must have been seeing it all along, not realizing that it couldn't be there. But it *was* there. He glanced at Gram. She hadn't said a word about the clarinet, but JJ knew that if he put it back in the attic, she would only bring it down again.

For Christmas, Gram gave him a biography of Benny Goodman. "Thanks," he said, and put the book aside.

The next day, when JJ was coming back from the heifer barn, he saw Liz sitting on the hay by one of the little hutches that housed new calves. What he noticed first was that she'd managed to get Jet's calf to lie down beside her in the sun, head in her lap. Jet's calf had to be the balkiest, stubbornest calf JJ'd ever had to feed.

He walked toward Liz, grinning and trying to think of some way to tease her. Then, by the way her head was bowed, he realized she was crying. He thought of circling wide around the sheds so she wouldn't know he'd seen her, but she looked up and smiled at him.

He walked up to her. "You okay?"

The calf lunged up and retreated to the end of her tether, eyeing JJ with her head lowered. That was more like it.

Liz stood up and brushed the hay off her jeans. "Did you know Jet's granddam was my first heifer?"

"And you bred her for feistiness, right?"

Liz smiled. She'd gone over to pet the calf, who now leaned against her leg.

"I don't know, Lizzy," JJ said. "I think you picked the wrong profession."

Liz looked at him with a strange, pained expression.

"You ought to be a lion tamer," JJ said quickly, and finally Liz actually laughed.

Later JJ felt very dumb, but it really was a surprise when Mom and Dad came into his room that night. He'd finally gotten around to cleaning up, and he was holding an arm-load of laundry.

"We have to talk to you, JJ."

Right away then he knew, but he had to wait while Mom hobbled over to sit on the bed, carefully stretched her leg, and laid her crutches aside. Dad half sat on the desk and folded his arms.

JJ watched them, hating their slowness and silence.

"No," he said firmly. "I don't want to hear it." He threw the laundry down, and kicked it toward the corner. "No!" he said again.

"Oh, J," Mom said, and the tears stood in her eyes.

Dad reached out for JJ's shoulder, but JJ stepped back and faced them both from the doorway. "You can't!" he yelled. "I won't let you! It's my farm, too. You can't!"

"We're not selling the farm," Mom said. "Just the herd. We'll still—"

"No! You can't!"

"JJ, please," Dad said. "We need to talk about this."

"No!" JJ kicked at the door to keep from kicking at them. The door slammed against the wall and he kicked it again and again. "No! No! No!"

Mom reached out to Dad to get some help standing up, but then they both looked beyond JJ just as he realized someone had come up behind him. One strong arm came around JJ's chest, and another over his shoulder, and Ray squeezed JJ hard as he burst into sobs. Dad came over and put his arms around both of them, and Dad and Ray just held JJ sandwiched like that until the heaving stopped. Then they guided him over to sit by Mom on the bed. Now Liz was there, too. She pressed her back against the door jamb, crying silently.

JJ leaned into Mom's shoulder as she twisted awkwardly to hug him, but she pulled back suddenly. "Oh, ow! This blasted knee!"

"But you said it was getting better!"

"It is, J. But if I keep—" Mom's voice went thick, and her face seemed to twitch all over.

"It's not her knee," Dad said. He pulled out JJ's desk chair and sat down, leaning forward with his forearms on his knees. He spoke to the floor. "I can't keep doing this, J, pretending I'm going to get back here while your mom goes crippled and your gram works herself sick, and your brother—" Dad swallowed hard and switched tracks. "This is bigger than we are, JJ—prices and markets. If it looked as if we had a chance . . ."

Dad didn't finish. He leaned over farther and rested his face in his hands. No one spoke or even stirred. The only sounds were made by Gram, still moving about downstairs. JJ imagined he could hear the little whimper in her breathing. He stared at the curve of Dad's neck, at the maze of white lines in the weathered skin.

Gram put on a record, and suddenly the clarinet quintet came coiling up the stairs. JJ squeezed his eyes closed.

"So," Dad said, and slapped his knee. JJ opened his eyes. "We'll keep the calves and yearlings," Dad said. "No better use for all this hilly land. So there'll be livestock— if there are any dairies left to buy it." He stood up. "And we'll still have hay, cordwood, syrup. We won't sell till spring, J. We'll have some time to get used to this."

JJ looked around: at Ray, now with his arm around Mom; at Mom, positioning her crutches to stand up; at Dad, going out the door and squeezing Liz's shoulder as he passed. Had any of them even noticed the music?

17

Night after night, JJ couldn't sleep.

It was impossible to imagine the farm without the milk herd, and yet his mind insisted on imagining it—in every detail, over and over. The heifer barn would be a lifeless hay mow. The milk barn would stand empty from April to November, and then they'd stanchion the heifers there under the useless pipeline. The bulk tank would be a huge annoyance in the middle of the milk room, and Dick would no longer come in his silver tank truck, leaving news of other farms as he took the milk away. Every July, Dick sold wild blueberries on the side, and Gram bought a case or two for the freezer. Would selling the herd mean no more blueberry muffins?

Every morning when the alarm rang at six, JJ felt as if he'd just drifted off.

"You look awful," Mom said when he got out to the barn. "Go back to bed. We're managing fine."

"So am I," JJ insisted.

Mom could help with the milking now, leaning precariously from one crutch, with her leg stuck out to the side. Ham had quietly withdrawn after Dad told him the news. The family would do this on their own now. It was just understood.

Right before the new year, the auctioneer came by—the same man in the broad-rimmed brown hat who'd handled Ham's sale. He walked with Mom and Dad through both barns, then sat at the kitchen table with them. Gram didn't seem to notice that he was still wearing his boots. The auction was set for the end of April.

"April 27?" JJ said in disbelief. "But Claire's not even due till May 1!"

"I'm sorry, J," Mom said. "Syruping will be over, but planting and haying won't have started—folks'll be free to come."

"But, Mom!"

"Besides," Mom said, "Liz has exams again in May."

JJ swallowed his protests. They couldn't do this without Liz.

Mom squeezed his shoulder. "You said it yourself once, JJ: there's no good time to sell."

JJ lay awake again that night, thinking about Claire up in the heifer barn, bulging with a calf he'd never see. Claire would be sold before she freshened, and JJ would never cross the line from farm kid to farmer. He would never milk his own cow.

He'd never drive the plow, either. Feed corn was only

119

for milkers. What was spring without plowing and planting? Fall without chopping corn?

April 27. How many weeks was that? How many days? JJ didn't want to know, but his mind insisted on doing the arithmetic: two milkings a day and thirty-one days a month, except 28 for February—no, this would be a leap year. The numbers spun crazily in the dark, but his mind plodded through the calculations several times until he was sure of the answer: exactly 238 milkings left, starting tomorrow, New Year's Eve.

JJ rolled over. Maybe now his mind would let him go to sleep. No! He forgot! On April 27, the cows would be sold after only one milking. That made 237 milkings left. And no more forever after that.

School started, and on Wednesday JJ took the clarinet off the piano and arranged for Dad to pick him up at Whitcomb's. There was no point in quarreling with Gram now. But school and jazz band seemed a million miles away.

JJ felt as if he were floating somewhere, watching himself sit at his desk or stand in the lunch line. His own hands turning the pages of a book or sliding a reed under the ligature seemed to move at an unreachable distance. He wished he could talk to Steven, but there were so many tangled misunderstandings that he couldn't imagine how to unravel them. For all Steven knew, JJ'd refused to get together out of spite. Of course Steven thought JJ was a jerk! And what if JJ did explain himself? What if he told

Steven about selling the herd, and Steven said, "Congrat-ulations!"?

JJ dreaded his individual lesson on Monday. It would be hard to fake it with Ms. Byron. As she sat down across from him, he moistened the reed and stared hard at his music.

She took a long, deep breath. "I heard about the farm, JJ."

Whack! It was as if all the distance instantly evaporated, and everything rushed toward him at once. He forced his eyes to stay on the music. He *had* to steady himself.

He felt Ms. Byron's hand touch his knee. "I'm so sorry, JJ. I can't begin to imagine . . ."

JJ blasted a scale on the clarinet, squeaking like a be-ginner. If she said another word, he would lose it. He'd either start bawling or yell at her. She was right—she couldn't imagine. Every single time he milked a cow, he was thinking about never milking again, and every single time he unloaded silage, he was trying to imagine what winter could possibly smell like without that spicy smell. It was *awful* at home, but all he wanted was to be there.

There was silence for a second. Ms. Byron's chair squeaked.

"Okay, JJ," she said gently. "Now play 'Memories of You' just the way you played that scale."

JJ glanced at her. She wasn't joking. She looked sad. He didn't get it.

"Just try it," she said.

JJ filled up his lungs so full they hurt, then pressed the

air out till the next breath came in a gasp. The music on the page looked far away again, and he played the song through without a mistake.

"You're too pale," Gram said that night. "Early to bed for you."

"I can't sleep."

"I'll fix you some hot milk. Have you tried reading? What about that book I gave you?"

The hot milk did make him sleepy. Maybe reading would help, too. JJ sat up in bed to start the biography of Benny Goodman.

Amazing. The guy had a million brothers and sisters and was really poor. Even so, when he was ten, his dad signed him up for their synagogue's band.

Benny Goodman was Jewish?

He was assigned the clarinet because he was too small for a tuba.

JJ was forcing his eyes to stay open.

Benny didn't even realize how incredible he was—thirteen and already incredible.

JJ turned out the light. Thirteen and already incredible. He rolled over.

That night after supper, Ray had gone out with Eileen, and Mom and Dad had gone to the barn to check on a new calf. JJ'd offered to help Gram with the dishes, but the only help she would accept was being serenaded. She had never said a word about bringing the clarinet down from the attic, but she asked him daily to play for her. That night she'd wanted "Ain't Misbehavin' " again and again. Now the tune was stuck in JJ's head. It snaked around all the real sounds—Gram coming upstairs, then Mom and Dad, snatches of conversation, water running and the toilet flushing, and finally the loud slap of the stiff old light switches. Then the tune spiraled right on into the silence.

JJ imagined that he could feel the very moment when everyone else had crossed over into sleep. It spooked him a little to be left behind.

But soon Ray's truck pulled into the driveway. The muffler was going on the old rattletrap. JJ was wide awake again, listening as Ray came up the stairs, clomped around in his room, used the bathroom. A light switch. Another light switch. Silence.

JJ hadn't been noticing that tune, but it was still there, swirling around the rustle of the sheets as he rolled over again. It was changing now, too, rising and spreading like smoke over a fire. He tried to hold on to it, but it kept drifting out of reach.

Suddenly JJ was up and dressed and padding in socks down the hall past Gram's room. She was snoring lightly, and he smiled as he headed downstairs. He grabbed his clarinet from the piano and went out to the back porch.

Sketch stayed curled in a tight ball on her bed and just rolled her eyes to look up at him. "You can go back to sleep, girl," he said, but as he put on his boots and jacket, Sketch got up and stretched, then followed him without enthusiasm across the snowy yard to the milk house.

JJ flicked on the light and went to turn up the gas heater.

He opened the clarinet case on the bulk tank and put all the pieces together as if there were some hurry.

The first notes of "Ain't Misbehavin' " broke so loud into the stillness that he stopped to peer out the window through the foggy plastic, half expecting lights to go on in the house. All was dark.

He tried right off to play that smoky music he'd heard in his head, but the real sounds didn't work that way. They jerked and plodded and squeaked. Maybe he should have warmed up. He walked back and forth around the end of the bulk tank, playing a few scales. Sketch looked up at him miserably, refusing to lie down on the cold concrete floor. He took off his jacket and gave it to her for a bed, but his feet were cold now, too.

When he went up the steps into the barn, Sketch jumped up to follow, hoping for some action, but all the cows were lying down, and even Sketch seemed impressed by the hush.

JJ dragged three hay bales into the milk house and arranged them so that he could sit on a stack of two and set his feet on the other.

"There," he said aloud.

He tried "Ain't Misbehavin' " again, but it clung firmly to the memorized notes. He played some Mozart, then blasted away at some marches from regular band. The room had gotten so warm that the bulk tank came on to keep the milk cool. This was dumb. He was wasting electricity as well as gas.

"Okay, Sketch," he said, "I'm calling it quits."

Just to leave his ear with something sweet, he played "Ain't Misbehavin' " again. He'd intended to play the simple tune once through, but it circled around again, and he played it over and over until it seemed to saturate the air. JJ heard it change, but he didn't dare listen, because he had to stay with it and see where it went. By the time it had swirled up and hovered there and spiraled down again, he was standing on the bottom hay bale and swaying his whole body so that the clarinet swung horizontal, then swooped back down close to his chest. He held the last long note and held it even longer, till his face felt hot. Then he cut it off sharply.

The silence seemed to tremble, and he stood for a moment, listening to it. Then he sat down and laid the clarinet across his knees. He rubbed the smooth bell, poked at the register key. The clarinet was a thing, an object made of wood and metal, but just now it had come alive. JJ felt himself grinning, and the grin got so big his cheeks hurt.

"All *right*!" he said aloud, and then stood up and shouted it. "All *right,* Felix John Jaquith!"

He tried to do it again. He tried playing "Memories of You," but suddenly he felt very sleepy.

18

January slid into February. Improvising in the milk house got to be a habit, but nothing changed at school. JJ'd heard a story about a tenor who sang beautifully in the shower—and nowhere else. He imagined Ms. Byron and the jazz band coming to the farm just to capture his brilliance. Saxes and trumpets would crowd around the bulk tank, and they'd cram Steven's drums into the corner under the breeding chart.

If Steven would even come.

For weeks now, regular band had been boring. It was hard to stay awake, but luckily, JJ could play this stuff in his sleep.

"All right, Jennifer," Ms. Byron was saying. "Not half bad. Now try to go over the top of those notes instead of sliding up to them."

JJ watched Jennifer play her clarinet. He could give her a few pointers if it mattered to him. But it didn't.

"Okay," Ms. Byron said over the noise between numbers. "Dig out 'The St. Louis Stomp,' will you?"

"What?"

"Uh oh!"

"I already forget how it goes!"

They hadn't played that number since the fall.

"It'll come back to you," Ms. Byron said. "Everybody got it? Just share with Hannah, okay, Mark?"

JJ pulled out the music—as if he needed it. He'd actually messed around with this one in the milk house the night before. He'd been up well past midnight. Fortunately, he just had to make it through today, and then it would be February vacation.

Ms. Byron sat down at the piano. "Jennifer, I want you to try this first solo, okay? And, JJ, you take the finale." A pause. "JJ?"

"Yeah, okay. The finale."

JJ moistened the reed. As Ms. Byron raised her arms for the downbeat, he stared hard at the music. He'd have to concentrate to keep from taking that first solo.

"One, two, ready, play."

Even with Ms. Byron pulling them along on the piano, they messed up several times. JJ checked the clock. He could play this blindfolded. The next time through, he closed his eyes.

He opened them, trying not to wince, as Jennifer wobbled through the first solo.

"Hey! Okay!" Ms. Byron called from the piano, and kept them going.

JJ closed his eyes again. As if seeing had been his only anchor, he felt himself drifting into a fuzzy, floating world. The sound of his clarinet carried him higher and higher, and he could hear the others playing, but they were far away. Now he was alone up there, with the drums way down below, steady, keeping him connected, while he swooped and soared and then hung in the air, holding that note as the drums got louder and climbed up to meet him. Just when they were about to reach him, he dipped, then leveled out. Drums and clarinet cruised in together for a landing.

There was utter silence, and JJ felt his fingers on the keys again. He opened his eyes to be sure. Clapping erupted from across the cafeteria. The principal had visitors, and they were all standing in the doorway. Ms. Byron stood up from the piano, smiling at JJ with a funny I-told-you-so grin. She put out her hand to acknowledge the band to the audience.

"Hey, JJ, great improv," Jennifer said, and other kids were turning around to talk to him.

JJ looked across at Steven, and when Steven started to smile, JJ smiled, too. Then they both looked away, but Steven played a soft drumroll on the snare and hit the big ride cymbal so hard that even as Ms. Byron dismissed everyone, waves of that brassy sound still trembled across the air to JJ.

JJ was putting away his clarinet when he felt something thump against his back.

He'd forgotten that feeling, but knew it immediately: the beater for the bass drum. Steven. JJ turned, feeling his face twitch from smiling to worrying to wanting to cry, but settling back to a smile. "Hey," he said.

"Hey, jazz man." Steven held up his hand and JJ slapped it.

"JJ? Steven?" Ms. Byron was standing in the doorway of her storage-closet office. "Can I talk to you for a sec?"

They hadn't quite reached her before she said, "I'm thinking of forming a trio. The West Farley Swing Trio."

JJ and Steven looked at each other, but Ms. Byron kept right on going. "Steven Lerner on drums, Felix John Jaquith on clarinet, and Cynthia Byron"—she bowed—"at the piano. Merely accompanying, of course."

She explained that in the spring there was to be a big regional band bash at the University Arts Center in Hampton. "Mostly marching bands," she said. "I think they need a little jazzing up. So what do you say?"

Steven raised his eyebrows right up under his bangs. "The Arts Center? I've been there!" He turned to JJ. "It's got like six balconies or something!"

JJ focused on one of Ms. Byron's gold earrings. "Spring?" he asked.

"Yeah. April," she said, and laughed. "Don't look so scared, JJ. That's plenty of time. We'll just do old numbers, new arrangements."

JJ watched her earring swing as she spoke. "April what?" he said.

"Oh, I don't remember exactly. Toward the end—after vacation."

JJ could feel Steven watching him. "Well, that's when—I mean, we've got something else around then."

Steven let out an impatient sigh, but Ms. Byron seemed to realize what JJ meant. She pulled a folder from a pile on the shelf. "I know it's on a Wednesday," she said, looking in the folder. "Yeah. Here it is: April 24." She held out the paper, pointing to the date. "Is that okay?"

Three days before the auction. JJ swallowed. Steven seemed to be holding his breath. "Well, yeah," JJ said. "That's okay, I guess."

"Good," Ms. Byron said, and closed the folder.

Steven came alive again. "The Arts Center! Can you believe it?"

"Hey, Ms. Byron," JJ said. "Wasn't that a registration form?"

"Yeah." Ms. Byron smiled. "Had to sign us up in December."

JJ and Steven glanced at each other.

"Don't look so surprised," she said. "I could've cancelled if I had to." She was looking for something else in that pile of folders. "So, is there any chance you two might practice over the vacation?"

Steven seemed to wait for JJ's answer.

JJ shrugged. "Yeah," he said.

"Yeah," Steven said, and he smiled. "I mean, it's a long weekend and we're going to my grandmother's, but then—yeah. Definitely."

"Great." Ms. Byron had taken out some sheets of music. "We're allowed only two numbers, so I'm thinking

'Memories' and 'Ain't Misbehavin'.' We'll feature clarinet on one, drums on the other. Sound good?" She handed them their copies. She'd already rescored both pieces for the trio. "Now hurry up," she said. "Mr. Prokopy'll kill me if you're late again."

On the bus that afternoon, JJ and Steven sat in their old seat, but they didn't talk much, except about the trio.

"I get home Monday night," Steven said. "And Tuesday afternoon I go to Hampton, but hey—how about we jam on Tuesday morning?"

"Sure," JJ said. "I'll come over after chores."

19

The milking was going more smoothly now that Mom was off her crutches. She bent from the waist instead of squatting, but she managed to be pretty efficient that way.

"Now," she said, laughing, "if my *back* will just hold out till April." She stopped on her way across the yard to stretch and arch her back.

JJ was right behind her. "Only a hundred and thirty-four milkings to go," he said. It was Tuesday morning, and they were headed in for breakfast.

Mom turned and faced JJ. "You're actually counting?"

"Yeah. When I can't sleep."

"Oh, honey," Mom said, and put her arm around him till they reached the porch steps. She still climbed stairs one at a time, like a little kid.

JJ ate his breakfast quickly. "Hey, Mom," he said, "after I clean the barn, is it okay if I go up to Steven's for a while?"

Mom raised her eyebrows, glanced at Gram, then looked at JJ again.

"It's just that we have to practice. Ms. Byron signed us up for this big concert."

Gram was pouring Mom some more coffee. "Concert?"

"I don't know, exactly, but it's at the Arts Center in Hampton, and—"

"The *Arts* Center?" Gram set down the coffee pot. "The *University* Arts Center? That place is huge!"

"Well, yeah." Suddenly JJ wasn't sure he'd got it right. "But it's lots of bands—all kids, you know, except Ms. Byron's in our trio."

"Trio?" Mom said.

Gram was pulling out her chair to sit down. "How long have you been keeping secrets, young man?"

JJ smiled and shrugged. He wasn't sure why he hadn't told them right away—maybe he still didn't believe it himself. "But, so, can I go to Steven's, Mom?"

"Sure. Ray'll run you up there."

"That's okay. I can walk."

"No problem, Squirt," Ray said. "I'm headed up to Ham's anyway."

A third gutter paddle had broken that morning, and Ray planned to salvage some paddles from Ham's empty barn and jerry-rig them to fit. Ray seemed in a hurry to fix everything these days. He was obviously getting ready to leave, but he hadn't mentioned any more job interviews, and JJ hadn't asked.

They cleaned the barn together that morning. When they set up the paper shredder, the motor kept dragging, and then a huge wad of paper would come flying out as the motor picked up again. "Drive belt's probably slipping," Ray said, but instead of cursing the thing, he stood with his leaf rake poised like a baseball bat. The next time a wad shot out, he sent it flying down the alley. "Home run!"

"Hey, let me try that," JJ said.

They used the shredder as a pitching machine.

"Fly ball."

"And he bunts it!"

"Stri–ike!"

Then they realized they'd shredded three days' worth of paper.

Ray laughed. "Hey, I'll take care of this. You go change."

Ray had patched the hole in his truck's muffler, but now it was getting loud again. "Hey," Ray said over the noise, "I thought you and Steven were on the outs forever."

JJ looked out the window. "Yeah," he said vaguely.

Ray started recounting a fight he'd had with a friend in sixth grade, but JJ hardly heard him. He still wasn't sure this would work. He hadn't talked to Steven about selling the herd, and he felt so raw he didn't think he'd dare mention it. If Steven made any wisecracks now . . .

Ray pulled over at the bottom of Hillcrest Drive.

"Thanks," JJ said.

"Sure, Squirt, but wait a sec. There's something I want to tell you." JJ kept his hand on the door handle. "I've lined up a job," Ray said. "Auto mechanic. In Hampton. But it doesn't start for a couple of months."

JJ formed a smile before he looked at Ray. "Great," he said, and got out fast.

"See ya, Squirt," Ray called after him.

There'd been no new snow for weeks, so the snowbanks were dirty and the roads were packed hard and slippery. JJ climbed the hill slowly. Maybe he could come right out and tell Steven: My whole life is falling apart. But even saying it to himself made his throat tighten. What if he cried? After all the distance between them, he sure couldn't trust Steven *that* much. Maybe they'd get right to playing music.

The Lerners' garage yawned open and empty. Steven's parents would both be at work, but still JJ went to the front door. He had to lean hard on the bell a few times. Maybe Steven had forgotten. JJ stared at the tile with the funny lettering until Steven finally opened the door. His hair was sticking up at the back of his head and his face looked puffy with sleep.

"Sorry," he said. "Got home late last night." He smoothed his hand over his hair, but it popped up again.

JJ stopped inside the door to take off his wet boots.

"Have you eaten?" Steven asked, heading for the kitchen.

"Yeah." It had been two hours since breakfast.

JJ carried his boots into the kitchen and set them down by the side door.

"Take off your coat and stay awhile," Steven said. He

shuffled about the kitchen in his bare feet, getting out cereal and milk. "You want anything?"

"No, thanks."

JJ took off his jacket and sat down, but he felt as if he had sand under his skin. He reached for his clarinet, laid the case open on the table, and started putting the instrument together.

Steven ate without speaking, so JJ could hear every slurp and crunch. When the sounds stopped suddenly, JJ looked up.

Steven was staring into his bowl, his spoon poised in the pool of milk. "You know," he said, "you could've told me."

JJ's stomach tightened. "Told you what?" He was sucking on a reed, and it waggled as he spoke.

"About selling the farm."

JJ grabbed the reed out of his mouth. "You heard?"

"It's a small town, you know. Dad said—"

"I don't really want to talk about it, okay?" He didn't want to hear what Mr. Lerner thought. To anyone but a dairy farmer, dairying at a loss had probably looked foolish all along.

Steven got up to put his bowl in the sink. "I just—" he said, with his back still turned. "I mean, do you have to move or anything?"

JJ almost smiled. "No way. We're not selling the farm. Just the milkers."

"Good."

It was as if a physical pain shot right through JJ. "There's nothing good about it, Steven."

Steven turned. "Oh, come on, I just meant—"

"Look, Steven. Let's not talk about it, okay? You don't have a clue about farms."

Steven leaned back against the sink and shoved his hands into his pockets. "How am I supposed to *get* a clue when you don't even tell me what's going on?"

"We haven't exactly been talking a lot recently."

"Yeah, and whose fault is *that*?"

JJ turned in his chair to face Steven squarely. "You're the one who hung up on me. You're the one who switched seats on the bus."

"Because *you* were being a jerk."

"Gram had a stroke, Steven!"

"I'm not talking about that."

"And then when I *didn't* quit, you still—"

"Look, JJ, I'm Jewish, okay?"

"And what does *that* have to do with anything?"

"You can't call the High Holy Days 'extra' holidays. It's insulting, okay?"

"I don't believe this." JJ's mind spun wildly, trying to replay that long-ago phone call. Had he said something about the Jewish holidays? "I really don't believe this. So that's why you wouldn't talk to me for months? Because I'm prejudiced or something?"

"Not exactly, but—"

"Well, I'm *not* prejudiced, Steven. I hardly even *notice* you're Jewish."

"Yeah, I know. That's what I mean."

JJ barely heard him. "So you were holding some grudge all this time?"

"Hey! *You* were the one holding grudges, JJ."

"*Me!*"

"Yeah. At the winter concert, remember? I asked you over, and you wouldn't even—"

"I was quitting, Steven. I did quit. Not just jazz band, the clarinet. I put it in the attic, but then—"

"Yeah, right. You quit. So how come you're sitting here with your clarinet? Same as last fall—you're just jerking everybody around. Give me a break, JJ."

In the middle of twisting the bell onto the clarinet, JJ reversed direction. "Sure," he said. "I'll give you a break." He yanked the clarinet apart and crammed it into its case.

"Oh, come on, JJ, this is nuts!"

JJ stood up and turned toward the door. "I told you, you don't have a clue."

"About what? Cows? This isn't about cows, JJ. I'm just trying to be friends. Who cares about cows, when—"

JJ wheeled around. "*I* do, Steven! Haven't you figured *that* out?"

"I just meant—"

JJ kept going. "*Sure* you want to be friends—when I'm playing music." He shoved at the clarinet case, still open on the table. "But those cows are my whole damn way of life, okay? So maybe that makes me weird and smelly and stupid, but that's who I *am!*" JJ was yelling now, and there were tears stinging his cheeks.

Steven looked stunned, but JJ's words kept spewing out. "This is killing me, selling the herd. *Killing* me! I can't stand it, okay? And you're asking who cares about cows? You call that being my friend?"

138

JJ was jamming on his boots and wrestling into his jacket. He yanked the door open and turned to face Steven. "I'm a farm kid."

With that, he slammed the door and headed, half running, down the slippery hill.

20

By the time JJ got down the hill and settled into a walk along the road, feeling angry was all mixed up with feeling stupid. What was he going to do now? Quit the trio? He hadn't even grabbed his clarinet, but he wasn't about to go back for it.

Why did Steven have to bring up the farm?

"Jerk!" JJ said aloud. He kicked at an icy clump of snow that broke into pieces and skittered in all directions. "Jerk!" he said again, but already he wasn't sure he was talking to Steven.

So what if Steven didn't care about cows? Steven was right. Cows didn't matter. Not anymore.

But why did Steven have to rub it in?

JJ zipped up his jacket and put on his gloves. He tried to focus on the sounds outside his head—the rush of the river narrowed by ice, the angry crunch of his boots—but his mind insisted on hearing again every word that Steven had said. *Do you have to move or anything?* There'd been worry in Steven's voice, but JJ hadn't been listening.

"JJ the jerk!" he said aloud, and then heard a car coming from behind.

As he stepped off the road, he recognized the racket of Ray's truck. He hurried down the steep bank through the trees. He'd walk along the river to the cow crossing.

At the water's edge, he held on to a small tree and leaned way out to stomp with one foot at the ice that clung to the banks. It was still too thick to break off. He moved along a little, stomped again, moved again. He stomped and stomped at the stubborn ice.

Jerk, jerk, *jerk*!

He made himself go over his own words to Steven, and now not one made any sense. His face grew hot with embarrassment. Steven had been trying to be friends again. And what was all that about being Jewish? JJ'd said it didn't matter, and then Steven—

JJ held still in the middle of a stomp. He looked at the flowing water. His mind seemed to somersault, then right itself with one clear, obvious truth: JJ wasn't the only one with a whole life separate from school. Steven had one, too.

Now JJ walked on without noticing the river. He'd known Steven for a year—a year and a half. Scene after scene crowded into his mind, and snatches of conversation. Synagogue, Jewish holidays, a few Yiddish words Steven had taught him. Was that all he'd learned?

At the crossing, the trees thinned and the river spread out shallow over smooth stones. JJ sat down on a rock in the sun and watched a birch tree that had bent low to the water and now was caught in a loose floe of ice. As the current tugged at the ice, the tree bobbed wildly. JJ felt like wading across and snapping the bowed branches so the ice could float away and the tree could stand tall again.

He stood up and went to the water's edge. Here the ice was thinner, and he could stomp off big shards and watch them sail away. The river was hardly a river—more like a brook—but he'd seen how grand it became as it flowed into the valley to meet the Connecticut. He wondered if that last ice shard would make it all the way to Hampton.

Hampton. He'd blown a chance to play at the Arts Center!

"*There* you are."

JJ spun around.

Steven was up on the road, straddling his bicycle. He held out the clarinet. "You want this thing or not?" He looked ready to heave it.

"Yes!" JJ said quickly, and his hands went up automatically—to catch the clarinet, or maybe to protect himself. Steven had every reason to throw it at his head.

But Steven parked his bike and came down halfway. "Here."

JJ went to take the clarinet. "Look, I—"

Steven went right past him to the river and started stomping off ice.

JJ set the clarinet safely on the sunny rock. "Sorry," he said to Steven's back. "I was being a jerk."

He thought maybe Steven nodded. JJ went downstream a little and collected a handful of rocks, cold even through his gloves. As Steven set ice afloat, JJ bombarded it.

"Did you really put it back in the attic?" Steven said.

"Yeah, and a lot of good *that* did." JJ threw a rock too hard, and it splashed freezing water back at him.

"You really would've done it, wouldn't you."

"What? Quit? Yeah." JJ threw all the rocks at once. "But it wouldn't have made any difference. Nothing would have."

Steven studied the toe of his boot. "You're right," he said. "I didn't have a clue."

"Yeah, but neither did I. I don't know squat about your holidays—or anything else." JJ shivered. "And the only Yiddish I know—*klutz, schlep, schlemiel*. Hey, maybe I'm just a schlemiel—can't do anything right."

"Oh, come off it," Steven said, but when they glanced at each other, they both smiled carefully.

Steven folded his arms, with his hands jammed into his armpits. "You know," he said, "where I used to live, maybe half my school was Jewish. And then I move here, and I'm the only Jew."

JJ felt a wave of guilt. He'd been too busy feeling lonely for being the only farm kid.

"Jeez, it's cold!" Steven said, and went to sit in the sun. He was careful not to bump the clarinet. "If I don't make a big deal of it, nobody notices, but then sometimes I get ticked off. I want to maybe wear a yarmulke to school and speak Hebrew in the lunch line."

"You know Hebrew?"

Steven laughed. "JJ, what do you think I *do* in temple three days a week?"

"I told you, I don't have a clue."

Steven came back to the water and started stomping ice again.

JJ scooped up some snow. "But didn't you just tell *me* there's no way to *get* a clue unless—" He passed the snow from one hand to another. "So what's a yamaka?"

"Yarmulke. It's like a little hat." Steven looked over and grinned. "Real cute, too. I have to keep mine on with bobby pins."

"Bobby pins? Really?"

"Really."

They both stared at the water.

"Sometimes," Steven said, "I hang out with this guy from temple, and I hardly even like him—I mean, he thinks jazz is a basketball team, for cripesake—but at least he knows what a yarmulke is."

"Like me and Lindy," JJ said.

"Lindy?"

"Yeah. She's in high school and all, but she's a farm kid—or at least she was. They sold out last fall."

"Oh, I remember. The auction. Lipstick Lindy, right?"

"Yeah. Lindy Hamilton."

"Oooo," Steven said. "JJ and Lindy Hamilton! Wait till I tell—" But then JJ's snowball hit him. "Hey!"

As Steven bent to scoop up some snow, JJ launched another snowball and hit him right in the rear. Suddenly they were both laughing so hard that they couldn't throw straight, but they stumbled around, chasing each other, getting colder and colder. The more they shivered, the worse their aim was, and the harder they laughed. Finally, Steven tripped and fell face first. He was still laughing, so he got a mouthful of snow. JJ went over to give him an arm up.

"Okay, now I'm *really* cold," Steven said, and headed up the bank to his bicycle.

JJ followed.

"So. Want to try again tomorrow?" Steven asked.

"Yeah. I'll be over right after chores. Set your alarm, okay?"

"Oh, don't worry, I will."

Then Steven wobbled off on his mountain bike.

21

The next morning after breakfast, Ray headed back to the milk barn to test his repair work on the gutter cleaner.

"I'll clean the heifer barn," JJ said, and took off across the field with Sketch at his heels.

This barn was built differently, with the hay storage at ground level in an enormous, high room, still called a mow. By now it was more than half empty. Sun streamed through the cracks in the wall, making slanted bars of light in the dusty air. JJ dragged a bale out to the heifers and pulled off the loops of twine. He loved the way the hay fell apart into batts, neat sections like irregular slices of bread. At least, after the herd was sold, there'd still be hay.

JJ shook a clump of it right over Claire's face, and she tossed her head and curved her long tongue to catch some. She really looked pregnant now. It was impossible to believe that by the time she freshened she'd belong to someone else. JJ rubbed the white blaze on her forehead and went back for another bale of hay.

Suddenly Sketch barked and JJ heard all the stanchions creak at once. Then there was silence. He went to the door of the mow.

Every single animal had turned her head to stare at the stranger standing just inside the barn. Even Sketch hadn't recognized Steven.

"Whoa!" Steven said, taking a step back.

"They won't bother you," JJ said, but every heifer kept an eye on Steven as he took one cautious step into the barn. "What's up?" JJ asked.

As if at a signal, the heifers turned back to their feed.

Steven looked relieved, but he laughed. "Guess they've never seen a Jew before!"

JJ smiled. "That's farm folk for you. Don't even know what a yama—what's it called again?"

"Yarmulke."

"Yeah, yarmulke."

Steven had squatted to pet Sketch, who was suddenly demanding a greeting. JJ noticed that he was wearing last year's jacket, old jeans, and beat-up sneakers.

"So," Steven said, and stood up. He stepped boldly forward, only glancing at the heaped manure in the gutter. "I came to help." He hesitated. "You know, so we'll have more time to jam."

"That's okay," JJ said. "I mean thanks—really—but you don't have to prove anything."

Steven grabbed a hoe that was leaning against the wall.

147

JJ was glad the handle was clean. "Sure I do," Steven said. "What?"

Steven thought for a second, then shrugged. "I don't know," he said, "but something."

JJ wished he knew how to hug people the way Liz did—just throw his arms around them and squeeze.

Instead, he smiled back at Steven. "Come on," he said. "I'll deal with the manure. You can finish feeding hay."

He showed Steven how to drag out a bale, pull off one loop of twine, then roll it to pull off the other.

"Neat!" Steven said as the bale fell open. "I didn't know hay came in slices!"

Early in March, spring arrived. The temperature rose into the sixties, and Mom practically lived in the sugar house, tending the boiling sap. Sometimes Steven got off the bus with JJ and helped draw off the finished syrup into the plastic jugs.

"Take one home," Mom said.

Steven and JJ were practicing together every weekend. They worked on the trio numbers, but they also messed around with old Beatles tunes, and with "Twinkle, Twinkle, Little Star." So this was what Ms. Byron had meant by "loosening up." JJ and Steven got downright silly. While Steven kept a steady beat, JJ would tootle off into the ozone, and if he messed up, he'd just play anything until he found the beat again—or burst out laughing. When Steven took a solo, JJ laid his clarinet across his knees and tapped his foot, trying to keep track of the beat.

This time, though, Steven was definitely lost. The bass skipped a few beats, and then Steven started hamming it up, tossing his head wildly and crashing away at everything at once, until suddenly he froze, absolutely still. He let the vibrations fade before he stood up to bow dramatically.

"Thank you, thank you," he said, as if to a huge cheering crowd.

JJ clapped. Then he started putting his clarinet away. He'd just noticed the time, and he was already late for chores. Only ninety-six milkings left.

Steven went over to his desk and rearranged some papers.

"So," he said. "We have this special—like—celebration when I turn thirteen. You want to play for it?"

"Sure," JJ said before the whole question sank in.

Steven turned around. "Really? I thought you'd ask me all about it first."

"Well," JJ said, "so tell me all about it."

"Well, you know, in Hebrew school, I've been learning the Torah—the Scriptures—so that when I turn thirteen I'm like a real member of the synagogue—a bar mitzvah, it's called."

"And you play *drums*?"

"At the party afterward," Steven said. He was obviously trying not to smile. "In the service, I recite the Scriptures—chant them, really."

JJ shifted in his seat. "You want me to come to the service?"

"Well, yeah, as a matter of fact."

"Do I have to wear one of those hats?"

Steven laughed. "You don't have to—but you can if you want." He pushed in the chair at his desk. "Anyway, there's a hired band for the party, but—"

"A hired band? Really?"

"Yeah. So we'd just be playing sort of a recital. My cousin and I are doing a rock number, and—"

"And we'll jazz things up!"

"You got it!" JJ'd held up his hand and Steven slapped it.

"There's a lot of Jewish music for clarinet," Steven said, "and my grandmother's got a few favorites. You mind learning one?"

JJ shrugged. Steven had played "Jingle Bells" during Hanukkah. "Why not? Music is music. How long have we got?"

"My birthday's in June, remember?"

"Yeah, but—you sure plan ahead!"

"All my relatives come and everything. Thirteen's a big deal for us. It's like we're sort of grownups after that."

JJ closed the clarinet case. He'd turn thirteen in July. If it weren't for selling the herd, he would have been sort of a grownup by then, too. "Well, see you on the bus," he said, but as he headed downstairs, Steven followed to see him out.

JJ'd left his bike by the front door. "Hey, by the way," he said, pointing to the tile on the door jamb, "what's that say?"

"The mezuzah?" Steven looked at the tile. "Oh. It says, well, those are Hebrew letters, one of the words for God, actually. There's a little parchment inside, with a prayer on it—to remind us of the Torah." He came out onto the step. "It's funny, I never had to explain all this stuff before."

"Makes it seem weird, doesn't it?" JJ still didn't know where "Come, boss" had come from.

"Yeah," Steven said, "but it's kind of neat, too."

"I know." JJ straddled his bike. "So say it again?"

"What? Mezuzah?"

It sounded like a sneeze. "Bless you!" JJ said, and left Steven laughing.

There was a week of rain, and suddenly the land lay exposed again. There were still patches of corn snow on the north side of every hill, of every building and every thicket of trees. But in the south sun by the front door, green spikes sprang up, promising daffodils.

Every morning, there were fishermen parked along the road by the river. JJ saw Ham's truck several times. The barn was still cold till midday, but the light lingered halfway through evening chores. The air grew thick with moist smells as everything thawed at once—the manure heap under the barn, the trickles of molasses near the tank, the spilt milk between milk house and calf hutches. Sketch sniffed at the breeze, taking such deep gulps of air that her teeth chattered. There was too much to take in at once. JJ felt the same way. He slept with his window open, breathing the thick air right into his dreams.

Every time he thought about April—the concert and the

auction—excitement and dread were so mixed up together that he couldn't even tell what he was feeling anymore: full to overflowing, like the rushing river, and just as tumbled about.

Seventy-five milkings, fifty-seven.

And suddenly April had come.

22

JJ woke in the early dimness and swung right out of bed. What had he been dreaming? He still had a tingling sense of soaring higher and higher. Swallows. He'd been dreaming of swallows—of flying among them, swooping and soaring. And far below had been the silos, like two silver buttons on the landscape. He had tried to keep the farm in view, but the wind had lifted his wings until the silos looked like tiny pinheads, and then disappeared.

JJ shook his head to get rid of the giddy feeling. He went to the window to see the silos the way they were supposed to be: huge and staunch against the dawning sky.

He was already dressed in a T-shirt and barn jeans when he noticed it was only five o'clock. He sat back down on the bed. What day was it? Wednesday, and— Suddenly the giddiness swept over him again. Concert day. It had actually come.

So auction day would come, too.

JJ went back to the window. The lights were on in the barn now, but the misty air was already pale with the dawn, and the birds were clamoring. JJ could see Claire in the side lot, standing half asleep. The white of her bulging underbelly seemed to glow in the early light.

Hearing the vacuum pump start up, JJ put on some socks and headed downstairs. Gram wasn't even down yet, and JJ found himself tiptoeing, as if only Gram could wake the kitchen. Sometimes she slept a little later now.

On his way to the barn, he looked for swallows, wondering if he'd heard them in his sleep, but they weren't back yet. He knew they always returned suddenly, but he couldn't remember when—soon? or not till May?

He walked toward the side lot to speak to Claire, but she barely bothered to turn her head. She was distracted these days, waiting.

The milkers had spent the warm night outside, and JJ could tell they were just being let in from the yard, because the big overhead door was down halfway. JJ ducked underneath.

Dad was coming down the alley behind the last few cows, and Sketch ran past him to greet JJ.

"You were supposed to sleep in," Dad said. "Butterflies wake you up?"

"Swallows, actually." But then Gert headed for the wrong stall, and Dad, Sketch, and JJ all sprang to divert her.

Mom appeared from the milk house and came up the

alley pushing the squeaky cart. Her knee was especially stiff in the mornings, and she walked with an odd, jerky step. Steam billowed into her face from a bucket of hot water.

She smiled at JJ. "This mean I can go back to bed?" She handed him the dip cup full of disinfectant. "Go prep Jet, then, will you?"

Around six, Ray joined them.

"Good timing," Dad said. "I was just heading out."

He handed a milking unit to Ray and came around to where JJ was spreading hay.

"Play well, J," Dad said.

"Thanks," JJ said, but bowed his head to hold down that river-rush of feelings.

He went inside early to shower and change in time for the bus.

Gram had made him a huge scrambled-eggs breakfast, and when JJ appeared in his good clothes with his hair slicked back, Gram looked him over and smiled.

"Maybe I should've dry-cleaned Gramp's old tux."

JJ laughed. "Yeah, right! That thing's huge on me."

"Oh?" Gram said.

JJ glanced at her, trying to read the wrinkles around her smile. He'd as much as admitted to trying on the tuxedo, but Gram probably knew anyway.

"Gram, can I ask you a question?"

Gram shrugged. "No harm in asking."

"Why did Gramp quit? The clarinet, I mean?"

Gram turned away. "Sit down, JJ. Your eggs are getting cold."

JJ figured she wasn't going to answer, but she poured herself a cup of coffee and sat down across from him.

"He didn't quit," she said. "The farm just took it away from him." She sounded tired.

"But, I mean—" JJ stopped because his mouth was full.

"When your gramp and I were married," Gram said, "dairying was a good living. It's hard to walk away from a good living. And he loved this place. He built up the herd and took pride in it. Do you want more toast?"

JJ shook his head.

"But I know what you're asking, JJ. That clarinet sat on the piano, and I knew he was yearning. He had a gift, and he wasn't using it." Gram stared into her coffee for a minute. Then she smiled at JJ. "You know, sometimes, late at night, he even—" There was clomping on the back porch. "That'll be Ray," Gram said, and stood up to pour his coffee. "Hurry up, now, JJ. You don't want to miss the bus today!"

All five classes from fourth grade to eighth were going to the concert as a field trip. The whole school was abuzz, and Mr. Prokopy didn't even try to get any work done. He took attendance, collected homework, checked that everyone had brought lunch, and reminded them too many times about "dignified behavior for ambassadors from West Farley."

Finally, the three buses were loading. Steven's mom was

meeting them at the Arts Center with his drum set, so, besides his lunch, all he carried was his music—as if he needed it. As soon as they were seated on the bus, JJ opened his clarinet case and checked again to make sure that he had extra reeds.

Steven laughed. "You nervous?"

"Aren't you?"

"Not nervous," Steven said. "More like petrified."

But he didn't seem that way. His face was flushed, and he joked and called to the other kids the whole long ride into Hampton.

JJ just wanted to be there, assemble his clarinet, play the music. He looked out the window, watching the hills smooth out into the wide, flat valley. The bus crossed the bridge where the farm's river spread out to join the Connecticut. Here there were acres of flat farmland, fields not yet planted but already pale green with new weeds among the corn stubble. JJ tried to imagine plowing one of those fields. He could practically drive all day before he'd have to turn around. Even in the valley, though, there were only a few dairies left.

"Hey," Steven said, nudging him, "we're almost there." He pointed out the other side of the bus.

In the distance, the university rose out of the flatness in a knot of high-rise buildings like a mirage of a city. After a few turns, the bus was navigating the residential streets of Hampton.

"That's our temple," Steven said, and JJ caught a glimpse of a low, gray building.

Suddenly the bus was among other buses, waiting in line to unload at the Arts Center. Everyone crowded to Steven and JJ's side to see the swarms of kids milling around on the big concrete esplanade.

"Look at that getup, will ya!"

"Hey, Steven, where's your feathered hat?"

"How many of those blue guys *are* there?"

Some of the bands had fancy uniforms and huge drums with a school's name printed on them. Some of the kids looked almost adult. JJ noticed one guy, taller than all the others in blue uniforms, who had hair to his shoulders and an actual scruffy beard.

"All right, sit down now," the bus driver commanded. "We're moving."

By the time the West Farley bus drew up to unload, JJ felt small and ridiculous.

Steven was a bit subdued, too. "Jeez," he said as they got off together.

Ms. Byron had ridden on a different bus. Now she sidled toward them through the crowd. "Okay, you two, come with me."

23

It was crowded backstage, too, but dimly lit, and everyone seemed to speak in hushed tones as if in a sacred place. Ms. Byron talked to a woman with a clipboard. Steven was to set up his drums where the number 18 was pinned to a curtain. When number 14 came off-stage, the rolling platform would be vacated for Steven.

JJ helped bring in the drums from Mrs. Lerner's car. As Steven set them up, JJ looked out at all those empty seats. There were hundreds of them, staring back vacant, waiting. He felt dizzy again, and sick to his stomach. He could dream about flying high, but in real time—now—in this real place, he would just fall flat on his face. He wanted, really and truly, to go home. He imagined standing safely in the yard and looking up at the silos where the guardian farm angel hovered.

He had only three more days to live on a dairy farm. What was he doing here?

Ms. Byron led them back outside to where the rest of the West Farley kids were eating lunch beside a long duck pond.

"You look pale, JJ," she said, and smiled. "Don't worry. You'll be great."

JJ couldn't smile back. This was all so simple to Ms. Byron.

He couldn't eat, either. Each bite seemed to stick to the roof of his mouth.

To make things worse, West Farley's seats were in the top balcony, and in this concert hall each balcony was forward of the one below. When JJ sat with his elbows on the front rail, he was suspended over the whole crowd, looking down through empty space on a sea of over-excited kids. He leaned back and swallowed hard.

"Scared of heights?" Steven asked.

"Me? Are you kidding?" JJ loved heights—climbing down the conveyor from the hay mow, climbing up the chute to the top of the silo. He just didn't want to be here.

Steven was studying the program and kept pointing things out to JJ. For the big bands, only the leader's name was given, and maybe a couple of soloists'. But for the quintets and trios . . .

"Here we are," Steven said. "Number 18." He read the whole thing aloud. " 'The West Farley Swing Trio. Steven Lerner, drums; Felix John Jaquith, clarinet; accompanied on piano by Cynthia Byron.' Jeez!" He folded his program. "Are you okay, J? You're acting a little weird."

Then the lights went down and the clipboard woman

came out to welcome everyone. Steven kept track of the numbers: seventeen to go, then sixteen. Some of the bands—even uniformed ones—were kind of squeaky and choppy, but others strutted around the stage with fancy turns and grand march music that got the whole crowd clapping and whooping. It all seemed far away to JJ.

"Number 9," Steven whispered. "Nine to go!" Number 9 was a high school jazz band with a girl at the piano whose hands went blurry in incredible solos. But it was real jazzy jazz, and the crowd got noisy and impatient.

By number 14, Steven was squirming in his seat. The blue band with the feathered hats marched up the center aisle and fanned out down the sides, and as they went up onto the stage, the whole audience clapped with the beat.

Ms. Byron leaned across Steven to touch JJ's knee. "Good," she said. "They're warming up our audience. After this number, we go set up."

Later, JJ couldn't even remember going backstage again. He remembered looking out from the wings and seeing—suddenly—that all those people had faces. The blue band was in the front row, with their feathered hats in their laps. The clipboard lady made a big deal of the fact that the next group had, "ladies and gentlemen, the two youngest musicians performing today." She even announced their names. But the moment JJ walked out into those lights, all he could see was Ms. Byron and Steven, and all he could feel was his fingers on the clarinet keys. What was he doing here?

161

Ms. Byron sat ready at the piano, smiled at each of them, and raised her eyebrows. Then she whispered the beat against the snap of her fingers: one, *snap,* two, *snap,* one, two, three . . .

Ba dah. Steven brought them in on the upbeat.

"Ain't Misbehavin' " was first, and featured Steven's drum solo. By the time he'd played three measures of it, the crowd was clapping. Steven's face got red and sweaty and his hair flopped on his forehead, and when he came to the final *bomp bomp crash* that brought the others back in again, JJ could feel his own heart lift as the crowd cheered Steven and Ms. Byron led them smoothly to the end.

When JJ turned to share in the bow, he could see that a lot of kids were standing up and clapping over their heads. Some were whistling. He glanced at Steven, but his face felt too paralyzed to smile.

Then Ms. Byron got very still, and the crowd hushed, and JJ took one deep breath and let it out as slowly as he possibly could. "Memories of You" featured his solo. He moistened his reed and focused on Ms. Byron for a second of complete stillness before her hand snapped the beat.

JJ played the slow, melodic part with his heart in his throat. If he was going to take off into the improv, he had to get his feet under him, push off from there. But now his feet *were* under him, and he didn't dare leap. He came to the last measure of the melody and started it over again. He felt Ms. Byron look up at him, and glances shoot back and forth between her and Steven. The audience seemed to rustle. They knew he'd blown it.

JJ closed his eyes and kept playing. He didn't belong here. He belonged on the farm, and that would be gone soon. He couldn't press down the river-rush any longer. It just rose and carried him with it, and he didn't care anymore where it took him.

He heard himself lift off right into the improv. The drums shuffled quietly and the piano was still as JJ looped higher, swooped down again, then soared on a note so high and long that he stood up from his chair but couldn't feel his feet on the floor. He trilled, hung suspended, trilled, hung suspended, then swirled right down to meet the rising drums.

He opened his eyes to the roar of clapping and whistles, but the audience went quiet again as he pulled them back to that slow, simple melody. "Memories of You" glided to an end with the undampened ring of Steven's cymbal.

Then the crowd seemed to stand up as one, and when Ms. Byron signaled JJ forward to take a lone bow, the clapping went rhythmic, and the audience was chanting. JJ bowed carefully, still unsure his feet were on the floor, and backed up to stand beside Steven.

"What are they saying?" he asked.

"Your name, jazz man!" Steven slapped him on the back.

Now JJ could hear it: "Fee*lix*! Fee*lix*! Fee*lix*!"

Ms. Byron made him take another bow, and as he

straightened and looked out at the audience, he had the strangest feeling: he did belong here. He was at home.

There were still a few people chanting when the West Farley Swing Trio cleared the stage to make way for number 19.

24

They couldn't be loud backstage, but Steven was literally jumping up and down. JJ couldn't speak. He just kept smiling so hard his cheeks hurt.

"All right, jazz man!" Steven said, and they slapped both palms together over their heads.

"You were great," Ms. Byron said. "You *are* great." She held out her hand, and each of them slapped and shook it.

The next band was a brass ensemble, and as it started up and the clipboard lady came off the stage, Steven and JJ calmed down enough to start packing up.

JJ was just nesting the last section of his clarinet into the case when he heard Ms. Byron say, "Oh, hello!" in her backstage voice. "I'm so glad you could be here!"

Mom and Gram stood in the doorway with Dad and Ray behind them. Ray had brought his girlfriend. Everyone was smiling, but Gram was grinning like a fool.

"Thank you," she said to Ms. Byron as they shook hands. Gram had her church clothes on, and even Mom was wearing a skirt. Dad was in his work jeans, with sawdust on his shirt. He was carrying his engineer's cap, and there was a crease around his head where the cap usually sat.

JJ had to steady himself to keep from running and hugging them all. "Thanks for coming," he said.

Mom laughed. "Wouldn't have missed it for the world."

"Fee*lix*! Fee*lix*!" Gram chanted, and shuffled in a little sideways dance step.

"Great job!" Dad said. "You, too, Steven."

They all stood aside as Steven's parents arrived. Mrs. Lerner paused just long enough to greet the Jaquiths before she went to hug Steven. "Wow," she said, and hugged JJ, too. "Fantastic, you two!" Then all the grownups stood around talking in hushed tones while the brass band blared and JJ helped Steven take down the drums.

Dad cleared his throat. "Well," he said, "back to work."

Mom touched Gram's elbow. "Have you done enough star-gazing, Dorothea?"

As Gram left between Mom and Ray, she linked her arms in theirs and added a little back-step to her walk. "Fee*lix*!" she said. "Fee*lix*!"

On the way back to school, JJ and Steven were celebrities. Practically everyone on their bus hailed them, slapped them on the back, told them how great they were. JJ got called Felix, as if it were a joke.

Then, as the bus left the valley and climbed into the hills, kids started singing all the stupid bus songs, and Steven sat with his legs in the aisle, bellowing happily in his new, cracked tenor.

JJ looked out the window, watching the scenery fly by like a movie played backward—the river getting smaller, the roads getting narrower. He was being rushed too fast toward the farm—toward tonight's milking, and tomorrow's, and too soon the very last.

Steven had wandered to the back. JJ could hear him joking with Tommy Marston.

"May I?" It was Ms. Byron, leaning over from the aisle. She waited till he nodded before she sat down. "You outdid yourself," she said.

JJ smiled, but looked out the window again.

Ms. Byron waited. "When's the auction?" she asked.

JJ swallowed hard. "Saturday."

"Oh, JJ," she said. Then she had to tell one kid to sit down and another kid to quit yelling, and she answered a couple of questions about how much farther it was, and whether the eighth grade would miss math time. But JJ could feel her attention still on him. "You've had a rough year," she said.

He nodded, still looking out the window.

"In the end, the music does help, though, doesn't it?"

JJ glanced at her and even smiled. "Yeah," he said. "I guess it does."

Ms. Byron looked beyond him out the window. "It's time you added saxophone," she said. "And have you ever thought about music camp?"

"Music camp?" JJ had gone all jumpy inside.

"Well, there's one out in Ohio in August—hey, come on, Jill, cut that out!—and I know they have scholarships, because I got one once."

JJ couldn't say anything. He was confused by how fast his mind had rearranged things. The money from selling Claire would be more than enough for a saxophone. And this summer there'd be no milking and no barn to clean; even haying slowed down in August—maybe he *could* go to music camp.

"I'll bring you some brochures," Ms. Byron said. "Steven, too." And she stood up to move on to another seat.

When they got back to school, there wasn't enough time for any real work, so Mr. Prokopy only had them clean out their desks before they headed home.

As the regular school bus crested the long hill, JJ turned a little in his seat to watch the farm come into view—first the domed silos and a glimpse of red barn through the trees. Steven was beating out a rhythm on the back of the empty seat in front of them. Just where the woods thinned out, Steven's drumroll crashed to a crescendo and stopped. There was the farm in full view. The woods and the fields were green again now, and the milk herd was out in the near pasture. Through the window glass, it all looked as glossy and smooth as a magazine picture.

JJ looked down at the clarinet case in his lap, and waited for the bus to stop by the mailbox.

Before he stood up, he and Steven slapped hands, then laced their fingers and squeezed. "See ya, jazz man," Steven said.

JJ stepped down onto the packed earth of the driveway, grateful for the manure smells that made the farm seem real again. But as he crouched to greet Sketch, he seemed to reach out from a distance to pet her. Something—not so solid as a window, but something, some kind of screen—seemed to slide between himself and his senses. He stroked Sketch roughly and let her lick his face, but her fur seemed too smooth, her breath too sweet. He wanted to *be* there, be home, but the harder he tried, the more separate he felt.

He took the mail from the mailbox and was halfway up the drive before he realized what was there on top: a booklet the size of a business envelope, with a fuzzy photo on the front. It was a black-and-white version of what he'd just seen from the bus—the farm from a distance.

The catalogue for the auction had arrived. "Edward C. and Catherine T. Jaquith DISPERSAL," it read, and then, in smaller letters, "Except for Calves and Yearling Heifers." At the bottom, just above the auctioneer's name and address, were the words, "This homebred herd has been very good a long time."

Right there in the middle of the driveway, JJ set down his clarinet and the rest of the mail to find the listing for Claire: "Lot 38 Butterfield Claire Annette 939824," and then "B.H." for bred heifer. It gave her birth date and the statistics about her sire and dam and their sires and dams.

Numbers. A long list of numbers. He could remember when Claire was born, how her eyelashes were the longest Mom and Dad had ever seen.

JJ heard the thin, stuttering bleat of a newborn. Then he heard it again—he was *really* hearing it. His muscles reacted before his mind did. He was already running toward the side lot when he realized he'd left his clarinet in the driveway. He went back to grab it and set it with the mail on the back steps.

"Hey!" he hollered. Mom was just coming out of the house and nearly stepped on his clarinet.

"Well, hey, yourself, Felix Jazz," she said, but JJ was already crossing the yard.

"Claire had her calf!" he called back to Mom.

He could see Claire in the far corner of the side lot, licking at a curled-up form in the grass. She had freshened early, and just like that—no fuss, no bother.

"All right, *Claire*!" JJ shouted.

But he stopped at the fence.

Mom caught up to him in her limping gait. "What are you waiting for?"

JJ was looking at his feet.

"Oh, don't worry," Mom said. "Your school shoes will survive." She ducked under the fence and turned to wait for him.

JJ looked at her. His eyes stung, and he shaded them from the sun. "What if it's a heifer calf, Mom?"

"What do you mean?"

"I'd rather have a bull calf." JJ couldn't keep his voice

from cracking. "What's the point of raising a heifer just to sell her for someone else to milk?"

"Oh, JJ." Mom came to lean over the fence and hug him, but in the middle of squeezing him harder she jumped backward with both feet. "Aah!" she said, slapping her thigh at fence level. "Zapped myself!" And though JJ could see tears standing in her eyes, she smiled now and beckoned to him. "Come on. Let's go see."

The calf *was* a heifer, and JJ was too much a farmer not to be glad.

That evening, as Dad stood up from the supper table, he told JJ to put on some shoes. "Let's go take a look at that calf."

"I've just got to clear the table," JJ said, but Dad had already headed out the door.

By the time the table was cleared and JJ got outside, Dad had disappeared around the barn. The sky was bright with sharp stars, and there was a chill in the air. When JJ got to the row of calf hutches, Dad wasn't there.

"Dad?" he called.

"Over here."

Dad had gone up the lane that the herd would take— no, *used* to take—to summer pastures. There was an old wooden fence along the lane, and Dad was leaning there with his arms folded on the top rail. "Look," he said as JJ came up beside him.

The slightest sliver of a moon was just rising above the hilltop pasture, paling the nearby stars. Most of the hillside was still deep in darkness, but here and there mist rose out of the hollows and trailed up to catch the light. Then, as the mist curled and spread, the light floated through the darkness in silver wisps.

"Your mom should see this," Dad said.

"And Gram," JJ added, but neither made a move toward the house.

They stood there, elbow to elbow, and watched the silent mist twine through the branches of a cider-apple tree.

Dad's voice seemed like part of the air. "That was a fine performance, JJ."

"Thanks."

"I wish your gramp could've been there."

JJ smiled. "Gram was there for two."

Dad was quiet again. Then he sighed. "I want you to know, JJ, I'm not selling any more land, and that's a promise. If things get better—if you want to dairy some-day—well, the land'll be here." Then he turned and smiled and put his arm around JJ's shoulders. "But, by the looks of things, you might be a famous musician by then."

JJ looked at the stars. "I could've quit, Dad. I tried to."

"So Gram said. But she's right. It would've been a sin."

"But I mean, back then I *could've* quit, but now—" JJ stopped short.

Sketch had circled back from scouting the hillside, and he called her to him, crouching to pet her. He couldn't say it aloud yet, certainly not to Dad: now he wanted the music more than he ever had—maybe even as much as the herd and the land. And *that* felt like a sin.

"I'm sorry, Dad," he said.

Dad looked down at him. "Sorry?" Then Dad chuckled. "You're just like the rest of us," he said, and there was pride in his voice.

Sketch squirmed away, so JJ stood up. "I don't get it."

Dad put his arm around JJ's shoulders, and they walked along the lane. "Well, let me see," Dad said. "Gram thinks selling's her fault—for growing old, I guess. And your mother thinks it's *her* fault for not wanting to hobble around like Ernie Adams. Liz feels guilty for leaving, and Ray—well, I admit I've blamed Ray myself. It would've been so convenient if he'd loved farming. But Ray's got a right to be Ray. And now, if I read you right, selling's really *your* fault, for being my father's grandson." He chuckled again, and gave JJ a squeeze.

Then Dad turned away, looked back at the moon, and walked a few steps toward it. "It's no one's fault, JJ. It's the way of the world, that's all." He took off his engineer's cap and stared into it.

JJ came up beside him. "Dad?" he said.

"What, J?"

"It's not your fault, either."

Dad laughed and put his hat back on. "I know," he said. "But thanks for the reminder. Now let's go check on that calf."

25

The auction tent nearly filled the yard between house and barn. It was yellow-and-white, just like the one at Ham's sale. Dad said the man who rented them had been in dairying once.

The chairs had been set up the night before, so when JJ stepped off the porch to head out to the barn, he had to circle wide around the waiting rows. The rest of the family filed after him: Mom, Dad, Ray, then Liz, who'd come home only the day before. Dad had suggested that even Gram might want to be there for the last milking, but she'd declined.

"Just fill me another bottle of May's milk," she'd said.

When JJ turned to wait for the others, he realized that the swallows were back. Some still sat on the overhead wire in a sleepy, puff-chested row, but several darted and chittered in the early light.

"Bet they're pretty mad about this tent," Liz said.

174

Five people made too many in the barn, but they all found something to do. Every cow had been groomed and trimmed and curried clean, but Ivory, for one, had lain in manure that was now crusted in a huge scar across her white flank.

No one seemed to mind all the crossing back and forth in the alley as they handed the dip cups or the curry combs to one another.

As the milking unit was removed from each cow in turn, Mom made some final pronouncement:

"Goodbye, Jet, you old troublemaker."

"Bye, Gert. Now, there's one sorry udder I won't miss."

"Aw, Ivory, you'll be someone else's sweetheart now."

JJ took over when they got down the line to Claire. Her udder was still hard, her teats still thick, but she had taken calmly to milking. "Goodbye, girl," he said. "You're going to be a fine, fancy cow."

The auction wouldn't start till noon, but the auctioneer arrived during breakfast, and soon the trucks began lumbering up the driveway, pulling empty trailers.

JJ eyed them from inside the barn. He was glad there were eager buyers, but those trailers maneuvering in the field still reminded him of vultures, circling in on the dying.

Then he watched the men and women who climbed out of the trucks and walked slowly across the matted field toward the tent. Creased faces, gnarled hands, gimpy knees. They smiled and greeted each other, but quietly, with respect for the occasion, like people arriving at Gram's church. This was a farmers' congregation, and JJ recognized that they gathered less to buy cows than to be together as farmers. Even the people he'd never seen before were familiar. In some indefinable way, he could count on them. He knew them, and they knew him.

Ray came up beside him and folded his arms on the next window frame. "See anybody looks good enough for Claire?"

JJ smiled. "Nobody's rich enough."

JJ saw Ham and Lindy coming across the field, and he leaned a little farther out the window so that they saw him and waved.

Ray waved back. "Hamiltons look like they're surviving okay."

There was a funny, hesitant tone in Ray's voice. JJ glanced at him. Ray was staring off beyond the river to the hills, his chin set so firm that his beard jutted forward. Ray. Always so resentful of the cows and the farm. He'd already started his new job, and would probably be the world's best auto mechanic, but this wasn't easy for him, either.

"Don't worry," JJ said. "We'll survive, too."

"Good," Ray said. He pushed off from the window frame. "You want to come help me make a sign for the porch?"

"A sign?"

"Yeah. Gram wants a sign on the porch. Anyone using the bathroom's going to have to take off his boots."

By the time the auctioneer cleared his throat at the microphone, JJ felt sure that every farm family the Jaquiths had ever known was assembled under that tent.

Now the auctioneer was asking "the folks responsible for this fine herd of cattle" to come stand up in front of the crowd. JJ saw Ray and Liz go into the house to get Gram. They were practically dragging her when they reappeared on the porch, but at the top of the steps Gram lifted her chin and marched past the rows of chairs without even glancing around. Some people were already clapping for her as she took her place between Mom and Dad. JJ stood between Liz and Ray, listening to the auctioneer's little speech without hearing a word.

"Let's give 'em a hand," the auctioneer concluded, and the whole crowd clapped at once.

JJ leaned back against the molasses tank, depending on its cool, solid bulk to keep him standing up. Dad took his shoulder and turned him toward the barn door. "Come on, J. Jet's first. You can help me bring her out."

Jet stayed true to herself to the end, balking and kicking and tossing her head. It took the whole family—minus Gram, of course—to bring her out of the barn.

"Guess she don't want to leave," the auctioneer said into the microphone.

JJ was glad she'd been first. He'd been so busy wrestling with her, so mad at her stubborn will, that he didn't quite realize till she was led away that the first cow was already gone.

It was a long time before the auctioneer got to lot 38. JJ had tried to eat a hot dog, but set it down after two bites. He went to put the lead halter on Claire. He rubbed her blaze and put his cheek to it. She smelled sweeter now that she was a milker. "Come on, girl," he said, and backed her out of her stall.

Mom walked with him into the auction pen. JJ saw Lindy leaning on the rail. He was glad she was there, but he didn't dare catch her eye.

"Number 38, ladies and gentlemen," the auctioneer called out. "Now, she's down in your book as a bred heifer, but she freshened early, and we think she's already milking maybe eighty pounds." He rattled off Claire's history. "Now, this is one fine heifer, ladies and gentlemen. Turn her one more time, and let's go."

At that, Claire raised her tail and plopped a curved trail of manure as JJ turned her. He smiled.

The bidding for Claire leveled off at $900.

"Hey, this is a fine first-calf heifer, ladies and gentlemen—years of milk ahead of her."

"Do I hear nine fifty?" called the assistant, and launched into that rolling jumble of numbers.

The bidding climbed to eleven hundred. Then it stopped. JJ stood there, holding Claire's lead rope.

"That's it, hon," Mom said quietly. "Let's go."

JJ's feet did not respond.

"Come on," Mom said gently, and took hold of the halter at Claire's broad cheek.

Still JJ stood there.

"Guess they want more!" the auctioneer called out.

"Eleven hundred and one!" yelled the new owner, and the burst of laughter seemed to break the spell.

JJ turned to lead Claire from the pen. The audience shifted quietly.

"You got a good price," Mom said, "and that was Francis Powers from up in Pownall. He'll appreciate her, JJ."

JJ swallowed against the rising lump in his throat. He led Claire back to her stall and ran his hand along her side as he left her.

"Hey, Felix!" The voice was familiar, but out of place. JJ swallowed again carefully before turning to face it.

"Hi, jazz man," Steven said.

"Hi. I thought you had temple."

"We did. We're back."

"Oh."

"Need any help?"

JJ took a deep breath. "Oh, man, do I ever!"

Helping just meant that Steven stayed by him the rest of that long afternoon.

26

When Steven had gone and Claire had been taken off in a blue trailer, JJ sat on the porch steps, watching the tent crew and the stragglers. The folding chairs had been stacked in front of Gram's flower beds. She had stood watch, making sure no daffodils got crushed.

Ham was still there. Ham would be there, JJ knew, until the last cow had lumbered into a trailer and been hauled away. Ham would be there until everyone else had left. Then he would go, declining Gram's offer of supper.

There were hours yet till suppertime—if suppertime stayed the same. Dad was even talking about trying to get some fencing done—restringing the wires that had been taken down for the winter. "I want to get those heifers out to pasture," he said, "before the haying starts."

From his seat on the steps, JJ watched as the nearest corner pole of the tent was taken out. Suddenly the whole front expanse of canvas bowed to the ground. JJ could see the barn again. The doors gaped wide at both front and back, so that light shone through the emptiness. Already, the swallows were swooping in and out, chittering with outrage at the disruptions of the day.

JJ went into the house to find his clarinet. Gram was at the kitchen table with a woman far older than herself. They were having tea in Gram's old china cups.

"JJ, you remember Mrs. Williams," Gram said.

JJ stopped to shake the dry hand. There was something familiar about the face, but he definitely didn't remember Mrs. Williams.

"Vera, this is my grandson, JJ."

Gram spoke loudly. Apparently her friend was hard of hearing.

"Felix John Jaquith II," Gram said forcefully. The older woman nodded. "*He* plays the clarinet, too," Gram said.

"Ohhh!" said Mrs. Williams, throwing back her head and then smiling widely. "Does he play in the milk house?" Her laugh was almost a giggle.

JJ looked at Gram. "Gramp played in the milk house?"

Gram smiled at him. "I thought I told you that. Late at night, so he wouldn't wake me." She turned to Mrs. Williams. "Sat on hay bales when the floor was cold, remember, Vera?"

JJ found his clarinet on the piano, but stood a moment, looking at the old leather case.

Gramp had played in the milk house. Now all Gram's comments about Gramp seemed to line up in JJ's mind:

Farming's what he did, not who he was. Dairying was a good living. It's hard to walk away from a good living. He had a gift and he wasn't using it. I knew he was yearning. Gramp had been a musician. He'd loved this farm, too, but he wasn't happy without his music.

And JJ had inherited more than a name.

When he passed back through the kitchen, the two women were deep in conversation again. He nodded at Gram's friend. "Nice to meet you," he said, and Gram was content with that. Her raised voice trailed after him as he stopped to put on his sneakers again: "Now, that son married the Coughlin girl, didn't he?"

JJ stood on the porch steps and shaded his eyes to look up at the feed sign on the silo. He'd always been glad that the corn-angel hovered there, always imagined that it was Gramp. Now he wondered how it felt to have wings but never take flight.

He looked around for Sketch. She had spent most of the day in the barn, following cows out to the auction pen, later out to the trailers, then returning bewildered to the empty stalls. JJ didn't call her. He didn't want to attract attention. He skirted around back, where the tent still formed a glowing yellow wall. A woman untying a rope nodded at him, but otherwise he wasn't noticed.

He was halfway up the steep climb through the woods when Sketch caught up to him. "Took you long enough," he called as she sped on ahead.

When he reached the hilltop pasture and settled on the turtle rock, Sketch waggled up to greet him. "Good girl," he said. "Now scram."

182

As he assembled his clarinet, he sucked on the reed and watched the barnyard below. One last trailer tottered down the driveway and pulled out onto the road.

JJ played some warm-up scales, but then rested the clarinet across his knees. He looked out over the hillside, feeling the breeze ruffle his hair. Why did the herd have to go on such a beautiful day? Cold drizzle would have felt more appropriate. Now the spring was seeping up into the sunlight, and nothing could hold it back. JJ played a few tunes, simply, then sat watching as the shadow of the next hill spread patiently across the river bend, turning its sparkling surface back to water. It was already time to be getting back.

He'd actually twisted the mouthpiece from his clarinet when his stomach cramped hard, and he doubled right over. *Getting back for what?* The barn was empty.

He thought he was going to throw up, but instead the tears came, and great gasping sobs he'd never heard before. The clarinet pressed into his stomach as he hugged his knees.

Sketch came over to lick his face. He grabbed her around the neck, trying to bury his face in her fur, but she squirmed free. She stood a few feet away, barked, then came back to lick his face. He pushed her away.

"You're a big help," he said, but at least she'd made him smile. He sat up straight and took a deep breath that shuddered out of him.

He put the mouthpiece in place again and turned the clarinet in his hands. Gramp had played in the milk house, played *this* clarinet. Had he sat up here on the turtle rock, too?

JJ stood up. He walked a few steps and stood still again. He shook his head to clear his thoughts. It was almost as if, for a second, he had *been* that other Felix, looking down on a thriving farm and feeling it pull at him as surely as if he were roped to it. If the farm were thriving now, JJ would choose it just as Gramp had. Eventually, despite Gram, the clarinet would go back to the attic. But JJ would never be happy without it. He was a musician—Felix John Jaquith—and he *had* to try his wings.

JJ ran one hand through his hair as if to brush away a thought that buzzed near him like a deerfly: In a way, he was lucky the herd had been sold.

The minute the thought landed, he brushed it away again, but as he stood there, the tears welled—not for sadness alone, but for the way that being sad kept getting mixed up with being happy.

JJ wiped his face roughly on his sleeve. "Feee*lix*!" he hollered across the valley. "Feee*lix*!"

Sketch cocked her head at him, and he laughed. "It means *happy*," he said to her.

He moistened the clarinet reed and played "Ain't Misbehavin' " several times. Then he moved on to "Memories of You." Before long, he could hear not just drums and piano but saxes and horns and trombones. They let him have the last note to himself, and he held it and held it until his lungs felt ready to burst.